MARKED PRINCE

QURILIXEN LORDS: A QURILIXEN WORLD NOVEL

MICHELLE M. PILLOW

MICHELLE M. PILLOW® - MICHELLEPILLOW.COM

ABOUT MARKED PRINCE

Prince Jaxx's inner dragon-shifter is at war with his human side. He knows what is right and what is prudent, and those two impulses rarely line up. With so many people in need and the planet in chaos, how can he even think about finding a mate? But when he helps to rescue the alluring Fiora from her captors, something inside him shifts, and all he can think about is winning her love.

"Filled with intrigue and adventure, Dragon Prince: A Qurilixen World Novel is an exciting new spinoff in a rich and intricate universe. Michelle Pillow creates characters to cheer for, to hope with, while building worlds that are portals for the imagination. Truly, Ms. Pillow is a master of futuristic fantasy."

Yasmine Galenorn, NY Times, Publishers Weekly, & USA TODAY Bestseller

"Michelle Pillow weaves a fantastical tale of dragon shifters, full of rich world-building, action and adventure, along with a sexy love story. This entire series is not to be missed!"

Bianca D'Arc, USA TODAY Bestseller

"Sometimes you just need to gobble up the insane goodness that is dragons, and Michelle has been aiding in that addiction for fifteen years."

Eve Langlais, NY Times & USA TODAY Bestseller

"A wonderfully sexy tale filled with romance and dragon-shifters that draws you in from the first page and doesn't let go. The Qurilixen Lords series is one you don't want to miss!"

Mina Carter, NY Times & USA TODAY Bestseller

The Playful Prince
The Bound Prince
The Rogue Prince
The Pirate Prince

Qurilixen Lords
Dragon Prince
Marked Prince
Fire Prince
Feral Prince
Her Lawless Prince
Poisoned Prince
Cursed Dragon

Captured by a Dragon-Shifter Series
Determined Prince
Rebellious Prince
Stranded with the Cajun
Hunted by the Dragon
Mischievous Prince
Headstrong Prince

Space Lords Series
His Frost Maiden
His Fire Maiden
His Metal Maiden
His Earth Maiden
His Woodland Maiden

Dynasty Lords Series
Seduction of the Phoenix
Temptation of the Butterfly

Having trouble finding the books?
Updated Buy Links Here

To learn more about the Qurilixen World series of
books and to stay up to date on the latest book list
visit www.MichellePillow.com

AUTHOR UPDATES

Join the Reader Club Mailing List to stay informed about new books, sales, contests and preorders!

http://michellepillow.com/author-updates/

Readers,

Thank you for your patience during the delayed release of this book. 2020 has been a hard year for many, including members of my team, and we all thank you from the bottoms of our hearts for your love and support.

I hope you and yours are well and safe during these difficult times.

Happy Reading!
Michelle

Fiora didn't want to eat, and not because she hated the taste of the unappealing green nutrient paste that they fed her for every meal (which she did). She stared at the injector tube set before her. At this point in her life, food was not about enjoyment, and she could choke it down if forced.

Instead, her stomach churned because she knew they were going to march her into a roomful of strangers wholly exposed. No, not naked—worse. Dignitaries from across the universes were coming to exploit her psychic abilities. Their questions would violate her mind. There were events she'd foreseen that she could not get out of her head—graphic images of unspeakable horrors.

Only she had to speak about it.

What kind of heartless creator gave a person psychic powers, and then made it impossible to lie about them? No matter where she went, she always ended up like some kind of oddity forced to perform tricks. She couldn't remember the last time someone wanted to just talk to her, get to know her without an ulterior motive.

If they asked, *Can you tell the future?*

She would have to answer, *Yes, I see other people's paths clearly but not my own. I call them timelines.*

If they asked, *Where do you get your gifts?*

She'd answer, *I don't know. And they're not a gift. They're a curse.*

Are there others like you?

I had two sisters. Salena was the luckiest. No one could lie to her, but she could mislead them. She was a humanoid lie detector and could make you tell all your secrets to her, whether she wanted to hear them or not. People don't like it when you can force confessions. Piera was sweet, almost too delicate for the world. She saw people's intentions in the present, like bursts of color and light. Piera would know with one look who she could trust.

Where are they?

I don't know. I can't find them in any timeline. I

have to assume they are captured or dead. Many nights I imagine they are dead. Death is a kindness. The universes are not compassionate to people like us.

Ironically, the only future she couldn't see was her own. How was that for intergalactic bad luck? If she could've seen her future, she could've avoided capture. Instead, she'd walked right into a trap, yapping the entire time about her potential use as a psychic because they kept asking.

Fiora didn't want to talk about her sisters, but that didn't matter. General Sten, the black hole of a base leader—yeah, she'd told him what she thought about him when he'd asked. He thought it was hilarious. General Sten pried endlessly into her childhood, into what she remembered from the night her parents were murdered by Noire townsfolk, who took her and her sisters.

What did they look like? What was the ship like? Where did you go? What did you see? What did they do to you? Describe how you felt as the blood of your mother dripped through the floor slats onto your sister's head.

Sten liked making her relive in great detail the story of three terrified sixteen-year-old girls listening to their parents' murders before trying to escape to the clay pits as the intruders set their house on fire.

The sick bastard got off on it. Literally. He grew a bulge every single blasted time.

Fiora picked up the injector filled with green paste and put it to her lips. She'd tried starving herself once. Being force fed by a Federation medical team had not been an enjoyable experience she cared to repeat. After much experimenting, they had found the nutrient paste helped her focus and made the premonitions stronger.

Fiora didn't want them to be stronger. She wanted to shut them off forever.

She'd found one way to mute the psychic images, but chandoo was dangerous. The drug flipped a switch inside her, speeding up her thoughts so nothing could get in. It sounded like a great solution —energy and no premonitions—but eventually, it would rot her brain and leave her a worthless mass of nothing.

Nothingness sounded good right about now. Then they could do whatever they wanted to her. She tilted her head back and tried pushing the injector past her tongue so she didn't have to taste it.

Fiora hated performing for crowds. There were so many timelines and even more questions. Everyone wanted answers from her, and they came with their endless queries and worries from every known corner of the universes. And if they asked, she couldn't lie when she answered. At best, she could tell a riddle and make the answer confusing.

When will I marry? Who will it be?

Will my son's ship make it past the black hole?

Will my daughter receive placement in the ESC?

Which path will earn me space credits?

Will I be happy?

How many blessings will my wife bear for me? Or will I have to dismember her to avoid shame?

Will I...?

Will I...?

Can I...?

Should I...?

Some of the answers they wouldn't want others to know, but still, she would be compelled to say them out loud, and then they'd blame her for their embarrassment. Even when they didn't ask the question out loud, she still saw the answer fragmenting through her mind. It was like a bad transmission wave she couldn't shut out. She could close her eyes, but the images invaded her thoughts. She could sleep, but they came into her dreams.

What she wouldn't give for silence.

The white walls were devoid of personality—unless sterile could be considered a personality. Federation holding cells were not meant to be beautiful. They were functional and easy to clean. General Sten insisted on calling her a guest, but guests weren't held as prisoners. She couldn't leave, and she hadn't chosen to come.

Fiora began to rock on the bed. She pulled the injector from her mouth and dropped her hand to her lap. There was no place to go. Eternity stretched on in the sheen of white. She'd seen enough lives to know there was nothing for her beyond this torment.

She missed her parents—the sound of their voices, almost like a melody filling her childhood.

She missed the color of dirt and clay, the smell of it on her hands, the way it lodged beneath her finger-nails after a day of digging to create dark lines across the nail bed.

She missed the sun, warm against her skin. Not artificial like what they pumped into her cell, but the actual sun coupled with the air against her body.

She missed silence but for the sound of wind in the trees.

She hated the white walls. They were too perfect, too clean. The white clothes they made her wear hinted that they wanted her to appear pure, untouchable.

But it was only a matter of time before he

touched her. General Sten, listening to the horrors of her past with his growing bulge and heated eyes, wanted her. She didn't need to be psychic to sense the danger there.

It never stopped. Fiora needed it to stop.

She missed...her sisters.

The sound of someone outside her door acted like a trigger. They were coming to escort her to the banquet hall. Her hand fisted around the food injector. Without much contemplation into what she planned to do, she acted, pushing to her feet to face the door. A guard glanced in, not appearing to register any type of threat. She had dealt with Rigger before. He always stared at her a little too long but never stepped out of line.

Fiora lifted her fist, wielding the injector like a weapon before tilting her head and plunging it into the side of her neck. She jerked it out, ignoring the pain as she then stabbed herself in the chest. Blood spewed on the sterile walls, painting them red and giving her some degree of pleasure as she weakly dropped to her knees on the white floor.

The life drained from her. She heard shouts and the scrambling of feet. She fell to the side. Wet warmth pooled by her body. If she could have lifted her arm, she would have pulled the injector from her chest and stabbed herself again.

Rigger leaned over her, and her mind instantly picked up scenes from his future. Fractured visions of a man and woman came with a soft undercurrent of music and panic. Rigger spoke to them in serious tones about a pleasure droid moments before the man knocked him unconscious. The images were faint, and her weakening body made it impossible to hold on to them.

Fiora would have smiled if she had the strength to move her lips.

"Get the medic!" Rigger shouted. His hands wrapped her neck as if to stop the blood flow. "What did you do? Blast it, Fiora. He'll kill me if you die on my watch."

Fiora stared at his face, unable to bring it into focus. Hopefully, his panic would be the last sound she heard.

2

POLITICALLY, WHAT THEY WERE DOING WAS
stupid.

Jaxx didn't care about politics. He was, what?
Ninth? Tenth in line for the dragon throne? And that
was if the elders didn't decide to skip over him should
the rare instance arise that he'd need to be king.

King Jaxx. The very idea caused him to laugh.
Hell, the elders wouldn't have to pass over him. Jaxx
would shift into his dragon form and fly away to abdi-
cate the second they tried to place a crown on his
head.

King Ualan and Queen Rigan, his uncle and
aunt, were fair rulers over the dragon-shifters, as
were King Kirill and Queen Lyssa, the neighboring
cat-shifter royals. But, for all the power those posi-

tions should have afforded them, their hands were tied when it came to the most crucial issue on the planet—the unwanted occupation of the Federation and their militant control over Shelter City.

The Qurilixen shifters called the settlement Shelter City because initially, it was to be a temporary shelter where the Cysgod aliens could heal after a plague had besieged their planet. *Cysgod* meant shelter in the old Draig language.

Qurilixen's suns had healing properties. A deal had been made quickly to save lives, and shifters had no say over the alien settlement. Though shifters could not prove when or how it happened, the city now housed more than the original infected Cysgodians that they'd agreed to shelter. It went against the agreement that had been signed when setting up the rules for the Federation's stay on the planet. The city was not meant to hold more.

If the shifters could prove the Federation brought more people to the planet against the terms, they could attempt to kick them off the planet. Proving it was difficult because they never caught them in the act of transporting additional people on-world, and they weren't supposed to be inside the city limits.

Temporary. The thought made Jaxx snort a small ring of smoke from his dragon nose. It had been thirty years since the Federation had tricked their way onto the planet, and now they refused to leave.

In the valley was an overcrowded marketplace and homes. The metal and stone buildings had been carelessly tossed together and were not meant to stand the test of time. Strips of canvas draped between decaying structures to give shade. This is where the Federation corralled their poor—which was any alien under their jurisdiction who wasn't conscripted into the Federation Military.

Across from Jaxx's perch on the watchtower roof, above the main city was the Federation Military base, and, on the very top of a ridge, political housing over-looked it all. The base consisted of evenly spaced, maintained buildings, a sharp contrast to the poverty below.

The large stone building which housed city offi-cials and high-ranking military personnel was set across from his watchtower but low enough that he could see the roof. The rectangular structure stretched along the length of the city. Metal arches slashed over the top.

Dusk had settled over the planet of Qurilixen. Three suns, two yellow and one blue, cast the skies in pale green. Since night only came once a year, this was as dark as the evening would get. Usually, that wouldn't be a big deal. However, to a dragon-shifter sitting on top of a cliffside watchtower with his giant body outlined against the sky for the Cysgodians to see in the valley below, it was far from stealthy.

And neither would this be...

Jaxx opened his mouth and spouted flames into the sky to signal to his cousin, Prince Grier, on the opposite cliff across the valley that he was in position as the lookout. In truth, Jaxx wanted to change places with his cousin. There was no reason the crown prince should be sneaking into a Federation stronghold in disguise.

In his shifted form, Jaxx heard the shouts of the citizens in the alien settlement below. If they had not noticed him perched on the tower's circular roof before, they did now. Even if the Cysgodians illegally left their city limits, scaled the cliff face, and then the tower, there was nothing they could do about his presence. He was allowed to be on the watchtower since it wasn't part of the *temporarily* agreed-upon Federation territory.

Jaxx hated Shelter City. He hated the smell of uncleaned bodies, the poverty and decay, the fact that the population starved. In modern times, there was no reason for any of it.

Decontaminators for bathing were cheap enough

and could easily be distributed throughout the city. Thirty years of constant sunlight had taken its toll on the structures, but it wouldn't take much for a work crew to replace the rusted metal walls and tattered overhangs of the homes and businesses. And food simulators didn't produce the most delicious meals, but food was food, and one unit could feed many.

However, the Federation refused to let the citizens have the means to materialize food because their scientists believed exposure to the minuscule radiation from the units would make them sick. Of course, no evidence of this was provided to the shifter scientists. The situation was a diplomatic nightmare. Shifters were not supposed to interfere with Shelter City, but how could they stand by and do nothing while people were starving. Lack of food would kill someone faster than a tiny amount of radiation.

Though Jaxx would applaud their efforts if the Cysgodians revolted and everyone fled into the borderlands, they wouldn't make it very far. But at least for a brief time, they'd know freedom—some of them for the first time in their lives. Jaxx knew that many of the people wished to leave, but they couldn't migrate beyond the borders without breaking Federation law, and the shifters couldn't take them in without breaking the Federation-Shifter treaty. If not for that, the shifters would have absorbed them into their society without hesitation. Taking care of your neighbors was a matter of honor. It was that honor that made them agree to the Federation bringing the Cysgodians there in the first place.

The political tension ran high, and it was only a matter of time before it burst, which was why Grier's decision to enter the stronghold to free a Federation detainee was beyond reckless. If he were caught, everything the royals tried to keep in balance would collapse.

Let it, Jaxx thought. *Things cannot continue like this.*

But he didn't mean it. Shifters might be able to conquer the base, but they could do nothing about the massive Federation army that controlled much of the galaxy. One fleet of ships and Qurilixen would be blown into a sad footnote of history. And the Federation had more than one fleet.

Jaxx stayed in his shifted form as he perched near the spire. With the armor of dragon skin covering his body, the chill in the air did not bother him. He focused his vision on his cousin and watched as he spoke to the guard. As a shifter, he could see clearly at great distances, but he couldn't hear what they said.

Grier stood at the entrance with his new human bride, Salena. They attempted to rescue one of Salena's sisters from Federation captivity. The triplets had been separated at a young age. Their unique gifts made them dangerous in the wrong hands. Something about Salena made it impossible to lie to her. Her sisters were more or less the same way. The Federation would love to have control over natural interrogators.

Jaxx turned his attention to the forest behind Grier and Salena, where Payton would be standing guard over them from the trees. He'd been friends with the cat-shifter princess since they were children. Payton was always up for an adventure, and they'd ignored several laws together—the biggest being the Shifter-Federation agreement when they smuggled food simulators close to the city. Someone had stolen one of their last caches of food simulators and were trying to resell them. He turned his attention to the valley. Payton had a source in Shelter City trying to locate the units so they could recover them.

Jaxx couldn't detect Payton, not that he expected to find her. Her father was a Var commander, and if there was one thing Payton knew how to do, it was hide from authority. He turned his attention back to Grier and his bride.

Salena's wore a tight alien-style dress and a different face, thanks to a morphing ring Payton had stolen from the cat-shifter queen's private collection. The morph made the woman unrecognizable. Jaxx was a little surprised Grier let his bride wear such a costume in front of the Federation men. Mated shifters were always on the more possessive side when it came to their women.

Grier was in his human form covered in reddish-orange paint. Tufts of Payton's fur had been glued to his face to make him look like an alien ambassador. Jaxx grinned. He knew where the white tiger fur came from because he'd cut it from Payton's shifted backside himself.

Salena gave a subtle gesture to signify they were ready. He breathed another stream of fire into the sky to let them know he'd seen her. A knot formed in his stomach. Now all he had to do was wait and watch.

Jaxx was a dragon of action. He did not like waiting and watching.

Somehow Grier and Salena managed to talk their way past the guard and enter the building. Jaxx focused attention on every exit. At the first sign of danger, he was swooping in.

In many ways, he preferred to be a dragon. Animal instincts weren't complicated. If he was hungry, he ate. If he was tired, he went into a cave and slept. If he was bored, he flew away. If he or someone he loved was threatened, he blew fire out of his mouth.

Simple. Easy. Instinctual.

As a man, things were more complex. Emotions became involved, and animal instinct warred with political reality. It was complicated, challenging, and filled with nothing but expectations.

And as a prince, expectations were even worse. He had to consider shifter traditions, Qurilixen's population, galactic politics, political doublespeak, the desperation of starving men, fear, treaties, laws, and on and on and on.

Jaxx could no more stop being a prince than he could change the fact that he was a dragon. Both were a part of who he was, and both informed his decisions. Sadly, like two warring personalities, they rarely agreed on the right course of action.

The dragon told him to rescue the people below. It was the right thing to do. He could do it now, and consequences be damned.

The prince warned him that such an action would solve an immediate problem but would create untold misery in the near future, worse than the current situation.

The dragon offered to fight anything that came at them.

The prince knew that such actions would result in the death of many, perhaps even the deaths of everyone and everything he loved.

And on and on and on the debate went.

Neither side of him provided a satisfactory answer.

Jaxx kept his attention focused. With each passing second, the knot in his stomach grew. There was no reason why he should feel so tense. Grier was a strong warrior and could hold his own, and he would not let anything happen to his bride. That is the only reason Jaxx agreed to this plan. Otherwise, he would've sent Grier home and gone in himself.

If Grier were caught, the Federation wouldn't dare to harm a dragon prince. They might try to keep Salena, but that would make for a very tricky diplomatic mess. The local general could deny holding Salena's sister prisoner, but they could not deny the existence of a dragon princess.

The knot inside him spread and turned into dread. Something was not right. The feeling had been nagging at him for hours. He couldn't define it, but it felt like a sickness on the edge of his consciousness, as if he were about to fall into a nightmare, as if at any moment his heart could be pulled from his chest and crushed into a pulpy mess.

Pain radiated in his neck, and he lifted his face toward the sky to stretch the muscle. It traveled to his chest, focusing over his heart.

The sensation wasn't fear, or panic, but a physical manifestation of an invisible attack.

The pain intensified, and he worried his heart might seize in his chest and stop beating.

Then, just as suddenly as it struck him, the sensation left.

Jaxx ignored the strangeness as he focused on the stronghold. His cousin needed him to be present in the moment, and whatever the pain was had lessened. His hatred of the Federation grew with each passing second. He would be happy when this adventure was over.

3

Fiora opened her eyes to the sterile white of the prison walls. Her mind instantly became aware of her neck and the slight buzzing against her skin. The pain was gone, the physical damage repaired.

She wanted the safety of darkness, not this white-walled hell.

Endless.

Maddening.

Torment.

Fragments of Rigger's future faded like a dream, and she didn't try to hold on to them. She didn't want to hold on to anything. The hum of medical lasers dulled the sound of voices, but she heard the whispers.

"Rigger's been stationed at the entrance," a woman said, her words clipped.

"I'm surprised the general didn't kill him," another answered.

They had brought an exam table for her and Fiora hovered over the floor. The mechanical whirr of a cleaning droid sounded even though she couldn't see the unit working to erase all signs of her blood from the walls.

"He still might—oh, good, you're awake." The woman who leaned in front of her view of white wore a stern expression, made more so by the natural ridges across her forehead. The irises of her dark eyes appeared to bleed from the centers toward the edges. "That was a space cadet move. You should be grateful you have a place here, and not in the stink hole city below."

Fiora knew it was useless to plead. She took a deep breath. Her chest had been healed as well. Too bad her heart still ached. With a dispassionate glance over the medic's stern expression, Fiora told the woman, "Your lover is not faithful."

The woman stiffened. Her irises became narrow pinpoints.

Fiora could have said more. She could have described in detail exactly what she saw connected to the woman's future. There were plenty of images in her head, changing now that the woman knew the truth. She had just saved her years of an unfaithful partner but did not expect the medic would thank her for it.

"Boost her and get this pet to her stage." The medic stormed angrily from the room.

Fiora felt an injection in her leg but didn't look as she stared at the pristine wall.

"She's right, you know." This woman's voice was softer than her boss'. "Things are much worse in the city below. You should find a way to accept your place here. It's not perfect, but you're fed and have shelter. What they ask of you isn't much."

The woman was trying to be nice, but her words were ignorant. What they asked of Fiora was everything she had. Still, kindness was kindness in this hell.

Fiora gave a sharp gasp. "Don't board the ship with the red stripe."

Her body tensed, and she couldn't control her muscles. For a moment, her mind was trapped in the second an explosion touched the skin of its victims, that first shock of pain before the nerves were stripped away. The boost they'd given her was doing its job, bringing the future into sharper focus. Each second played out like an eternity.

This was her life.

No, her life was seeing *their* lives.

It never ended.

When Fiora's thoughts returned from the space crash, she was alone in the room. She pushed up from the exam table. Someone had changed her clothes, dressing her in the white tunic shirt and pants. A white cap had been placed next to her, along with a hair tie. She didn't fight what had to be done. She brushed her fingers through her hair and pulled the length high on her head before placing the cap over the top.

This time when they came for her, she did not resist. She kept her eyes down, focusing on trying to keep out all the emotions she could. She watched the feet of the men in black uniforms as they walked on either side of her. In her mind, she built a brick wall around her body. It floated with her, pushing the timelines away like a battering ram. It worked for a short time, but when they passed into a large banquet hall, as white and sterile as the rest of the building, the sound of guests rushing over her like a waterfall. Their lives wore at the mortar and chipped at the bricks, cracking holes for images to leak through.

Uniformed soldiers walked past with trays of food to act the part of the servants. General Sten did not want any other locals roaming the base so the duties were regulated to the newest recruits. He was right to keep the Cysgodians at a distance though his ego would hardly let him admit to fearing anyone in the city below.

The arrogance in the room hung thick in the air and made her feel like a tiny star surrounded by endless sky. Close to a hundred alien dignitaries from around the universes crowded the hall, each secretly fighting for dominance even as they smiled and made small talk. The murmur of voices became indistinguishable beyond a drone of noise backdropped by soft music.

Fiora felt her neck where she'd stabbed herself. There wasn't even a scar to mark her attempt. It was as if it hadn't happened. For some reason that made her sad. As if she were nothing and her will held no permanence in this lifetime.

She wanted them to see her pain. Maybe one of them would take pity on her if they knew the torment that she faced in being here. Then again, from what she saw of their lives, such salvation was doubtful in this crowd.

Fiora lifted her gaze, trying to find someone who

would end her life. A transparent figure drew her attention. The G'am man stood naked as if to show off the stunning pattern created by the blood vessels beneath his skin. She saw a future in which he was telling someone they were his glory. His organs pulsed. He appeared too thin and willowy to do much damage, but the Dokka trader he talked to might do the job. Then there was the furry Lykan. He had anger in him, boiling beneath the surface. It wouldn't take much to stir him to rage. Or perhaps the reptilian Slit'therne. Or, maybe still, any number of the humanoid creatures. Many of the people here had murder in them. If she found the right temper, embarrassed them with the right secret, then maybe...

Fiora frowned.

A chill worked its way through her, and she was struck with the memory of clay pits in the moonlight. It brought with it a rush of feelings. The clay pits were home. She used to lay in them with her sisters. She hadn't felt safe since childhood when the darkness surrounded her and kept her out of the light. The sensation moved over her like an electrical current to center on her chest. "Who?"

Fiora looked around, searching the crowd. She hadn't felt that particular impression since she'd last been with her sisters. But as she gazed from face to face, it was too much to hope that she would see them again. Salena and Piera were not there.

"Keep walking," her guard ordered, nudging her lightly in the back.

Fiora found General Sten in the crowd. If he had not been in a position of power, there would be nothing remarkable about the man. He did not have a memorable face, a distinctive voice, or a particularly frightening natural demeanor. The general's gaze found hers. He smiled, but the look did not reach his cold eyes, as if he willed her to see the future that he had planned for her. Not surprisingly, no images came to her. She did not see her own timeline.

"Come on," the guard grumbled. This one wasn't typically so abrupt with her, but she imagined he'd heard the trouble Rigger had gotten into because of her. She tried to remember the soldier's name, but it was lost as visions flew at her from the crowd.

She made her way to a large chair on a platform. The eyes of those gathered found her as if by taking a seat she indicated to them that the show was about to begin. Their silent questions came at her, held together with anticipation and worry. The people inched closer. Timelines rushed in, fighting for attention within the small confines of her brain. A dull ache started in her temple and would only grow worse as the evening progressed.

She closed her eyes, trying to block them out.

Taw. The guard's name was Taw. She saw him standing rigid and alone through banquets just like this one, an endless destiny of undistinguished service.

"I would ask you all to back away," Taw said, the perfunctory tone of his voice revealing to anyone who cared to notice that this was not the first time he'd gone through the rules. "Prepare your *one* question carefully. You only get one so that everyone may have a chance. There will be no touching while she employs her second sight."

Employ? Like it was a choice? Like she could choose to unemploy it?

She caught a vision of one of the dignitaries in a future chandoo trade and desperately wondered if he was carrying any now. The guard kept going through his list of rules. She ignored him. So would half the people here.

Taw ended his speech, but she didn't want to open her eyes. The visions became more substantial, and she wondered what they'd given her in the injection. She wouldn't put it past the general to order that she be given an extra-strong dose as a punishment.

"Yes, you, go on," Taw said. "Ask your question."

A nervous giggle sounded before a hesitant voice asked, "Will I...? When will I...?"

Fiora opened one eye to look at the woman briefly. The light stung, making the growing headache worse. Normally a crowd this size would cause her nose to start bleeding, but the doctors had found a temporary way of stopping it with medicine.

"When will my husband and I have a baby?" she asked. The man standing next to her widened his eyes, slightly alarmed.

Fiora closed her eyes, and she was compelled to find the answer to the question. "Fruit will not grow where there is no tree."

A murmur of voices came from the crowd as people commented on the answer amongst themselves.

"I don't understand," the woman complained.

Fiora could have told the woman that she needed to get married first to have a husband, and that she couldn't have a baby with a husband until that happened, and the man she was with was not going to marry her. She could have also told the woman that she would get pregnant, but that man would be married to someone else.

Fiora preferred being cryptic in her response.

"What—?" the mistress tried to protest.

"Next." Taw cut off the woman's second question.

"Who will win this year's Galactic Crown?" The words slurred together into one long, continuous sound, lacking enunciation.

Fiora pictured a drunken man holding tight to a betting chip as he stared at a viewing screen in a seedy ship casino. "Three gray eyes and forty brown will see a victory in black."

"Three gray, forty brown," the man repeated softly. "Three gray, forty brown."

"Where is my grandmother's heart?" asked a Slit'therne noble.

At the same time, another man announced, "This is a hoax. Anyone can make up riddles. I expected better of the Federation."

Fiora was grateful that the doubting man didn't ask her a question about his future. He didn't have much of one. Timelines continued to come at her, bolder than before.

"Where is my grandmother's heart?" the impatient Slit'therne demanded a second time. Aggression filled his words.

Fiora felt a shiver work over her body and forced her eyes to open. The Slit'therne were a snake-like race often found building their nests in boggy locales. The upper half of the man's body was humanoid in basic shape, green-yellow scales covered his flesh, and his hands were webbed. A thick tail replaced what would have been humanoid legs.

"After the moon sets for the last time, you will journey to a tree, and there you will find the key to your victory," Fiora told the Slit'therne. He wouldn't like the answer, but that was too bad.

When it looked like the man would protest, Taw stepped forward in warning. The Slit'therne propelled himself backward on his tail.

Fiora wanted to scream. The harder they stared, the stronger their lives invaded her, shriveling pieces of her soul to make room. She glanced over the crowd, thinking with despair of how long it would take her to get through all of them.

It never ended.

"Next," Taw said.

There was murmuring, but no one readily spoke.

"Next," the guard repeated, lifting his arm

toward a Lykan male to make an arbitrary choice amongst those watching.

The Lykan's fur had been combed flat and fixed into place so that it barely moved. His voice was gruff as he commanded, "What of my wife?"

Fiora frowned and closed her eyes to concentrate. She opened them just as quickly. "You don't have a wife."

The Lykan stiffened, and she was sure his fur would have bristled if it could have moved. A tiny growl sounded in the back of his throat.

She held up her hands to stop his anger and closed her eyes to take a more in-depth look. The headache made it hard to think of a riddle. "I see a bride in your future. Two space years."

He grunted and nodded, stepping back. She knew he'd be pleased by this news.

A new timeline surged to the forefront, bringing with it a blast of heat that prickled her nerves. Fiora inhaled sharply. She envisioned a man's body ripping apart as a giant monster emerged from inside his flesh. The sound of screams echoed, and fires erupted all around her. The crowd did not react to the flames as the vision overlapped reality.

A man with reddish-orange skin and tufts of white fur on his face pushed his way to the front of the crowd. The mistress wanting a baby tried to take a second turn, but the new alien stopped her by grabbing the back of her arm and tugging her aside. The fiery images seemed to be coming from him, but he looked nothing like the monster in her vision. She didn't recognize the alien creature.

Reaching behind him, he pulled a human woman forward as if she was the real reason that he'd put himself at the front of the gathering. Fiora didn't recognize the woman. A tight dress hugged her generous curves, and her face looked as if it had been subjected to the inept laser of a second-tier MAPH surgeon. The Medical Alliance for Planetary Health had a monopoly on all things medical.

The flames died down to a quiet shimmer in the background of her thoughts. Yes, she had a headache and was bombarded with futures, but when she focused on the woman, she should have picked up more than blurry facial features and the sound of a bone cracking.

The woman reached for her with shaking hands, as if she was both afraid and eager. Fiora stiffened and concentrated harder. The woman's timeline refused to come into focus.

"Don't touch," Taw warned.

Fiora lifted a hand to stop him from pushing the woman back. "No, it's all right. She won't hurt me."

Fiora didn't know why she thought so, but if she said the words, then they had to be true. Maybe the boost injection was affecting her concentration. Taw hesitated before finally stepping back and motioning the stranger to approach.

The woman took Fiora's hand. A shiver worked up her arm, a familiar tug that went against all she was seeing before her. There were only two people in the entire universes who could send that particular awareness through her body.

Fiora's breath caught in her throat, and she wasn't sure she could allow herself to think it. The woman standing before her could not be her sister. Unless...the second-tier surgeon? Had someone destroyed one of her sisters' faces? Her body?

Piera? Salena?

Fiora gripped the hand tighter, not wanting to let go. She waited for the woman to speak, to end the mystery.

"You poor thing," the woman said in a high-pitched whine. The voice was not familiar. "I have seen fortune-tellers before. You look as if you need a break."

"That's enough," Taw interrupted. "Step back."

Fiora let the weakness take her, and she swayed on the seat. She needed to know more and couldn't do it in front of the crowd. If General Sten suspected another of the triplets were here, he'd imprison them both. "I think she's right. The images become clearer when I am rested. I need a small break. There are too many futures in this room."

The woman stepped back, and Fiora called out before she could become swallowed by the crowd. "Don't you want your prediction?"

The woman nodded.

"You will find what you are looking for," Fiora said, hoping to send some kind of message to her.

The woman smiled and continued to back away. "Thank you."

Fiora lost sight of her. She stood and purposefully swayed on her feet. So the crowd could hear her, she said, "I must excuse myself for a moment." Then to Taw, she added, "The shot they gave me has left me feeling strange." She gave a meaningful glance downward.

Taw nodded, gesturing that she should walk with him. When they left the banquet room, she quickened her pace to keep them from asking her any questions. At the end of the long hall, she slipped into a comfort room and gestured for the guards to stay back. Taw ignored her, going inside to make sure the place was empty before leaving her alone.

Fiora pressed her fist against her chest. Her heart physically ached. She tried to calm her breathing, but it was difficult.

Why was she feeling her sister? For years she'd searched every crowd looking for faces like her own. Well, like her own minus the scar on her forehead she'd received the night they were forced from their loving home.

"Turn around," Taw announced from the other side of the door. "This area is closed."

A strange grunt followed his words. Taw moaned in pain.

Fiora moved closer to the door to hear what was being said. She detected a series of thumps.

"I think rendering him unconscious is actually a kindness," a man said on the other side of the door.

Fiora backed away from the door and watched it open. The woman in the tight dress appeared. Behind her, Taw and the other guard were unconscious on the floor. The man with the furry face stood over them.

"Who are you?" Fiora demanded as she stared at the woman's face.

The woman lifted her hand and fidgeted with

the ring on her finger. Her skin began to stretch and contract. Fiora gasped at the strange sight and placed her hand to her throat as if the gesture would help her breathe.

The woman jerked the ring off her finger and slapped more than handed the jewelry to the man with her. Her body shape changed as she came for Fiora, arms widespread.

Fiora gasped as the woman hugged her, her face morphing into one more familiar as she moved. Shaking, she whispered, "Salena? I didn't know if I could believe it. How?"

"There will be time for questions later," the man stated. "We have to figure out a way to get you out of here."

Fiora looked at him, eyeing the strange markings on his face. They didn't fit the visions she had when she looked into his future. Was he in disguise as well? She looked at his hands, trying to see if there was a similar ring device.

"It's all right." Salena tried to reassure her. "This is—"

"No. Don't tell me." Fiora shook her head.

Panic set in as she looked at her sister. A sense of urgency filled her, ruining any happiness that should have erupted at their reunion. All of the tender sentiments she would have said in such a moment vanished. For so long, all she wanted was to be reunited with Piera and Salena. They were the missing pieces of her soul and seeing one piece brought back to her should have been a reason for joy. But not here. Not like this. The Federation base was too dangerous. As much as she hated her fate, it would be worse to see a sister going through the same nightmare as well.

"You shouldn't have come. I can't leave here. If I don't show back up soon, they will send people after me. They will find me. And, if they ask me who you are, I'll have to tell them because I cannot lie. So don't tell me anything more. Just put that face back on and get out of here. I'll give them so many predictions they won't think to ask me about you." Fiora knew if she went back to the hall and started telling predictions, they wouldn't sound an alarm. She tried to move past the man blocking the exit.

Salena stopped her. "Grier, hide those men. We don't want to draw suspicions if anyone looks this way."

Grier nodded and left to do as Salena bid.

When they were alone, Salena said, "Take your clothes off. I have a plan."

Fiora made no move to follow the orders. This

was not like when they were children, and Salena got to play the role of bossy triplet. "Salena, wh—?"

"You can't lie, but I can," Salena explained. Her ability made people tell her the truth. Fiora could easily admit she'd envied it most of her life. "We're going to change places. I'm going to tell fortunes, and you're going to walk out of here dressed as a pleasure droid bimbo."

This was a bad plan.

Fiora shook her head in denial even as Salena began stripping. "What about you? That means you'll be stuck here. I can't do that. I can't leave you here. They're going to realize eventually that you can't do what I do. You don't know what it's like to be locked in a cage by the Federation."

She thought of all the times General Sten had come to her prison hold to listen to her torments. Then there were the shots and tests. And the horrible nutrient paste they forced her to eat.

"I'm a toy to them," Fiora stated.

"I *do* know what it's like. I'm here because the Federation brought me. They came for both of us. I was lucky enough to escape." Salena finally managed to wiggle out of her tight clothes. "And that man with me is my husband. He's a prince on this planet. If anyone can protect us, it is him and his family."

Salena stood before her naked. Fiora didn't move.

Salena attempted to hand her the dress. "I'm here to rescue you. You're coming with us. My lies will create a distraction in there. And once started, you know they will not be able to resist telling each other the truth."

Fiora wondered if her sister's ability had grown over their years apart. It would make sense. If Salena asked someone a question, they were compelled to speak truthfully. But it didn't stop there. It sometimes spread like a virus. The arguing would build when the infected became so entrenched in their anger that they mindlessly fed off each other's emotions. The truth-telling would become its own force, stirred by churning emotions.

"I have a feeling that crowd has a lot of secrets they do not want to be told," Salena continued. "I also assume they have strong opinions about some of their fellow partygoers that they will be only too willing to share. You can't have that many alien races in one room without someone holding a grudge or feeling superior."

She again tried to hand over the dress.

Fiora again refused to take it. She saw the stubbornness in her sister's expression. "You haven't changed."

"Yes, I have. I will not hesitate again." Salena shook the dress insistently. "Now hurry."

Fiora knew there was no point in arguing with her. She pulled her shirt over her head and thrust it at her sister. "Is Piera with you?"

"No. I hoped you knew something about her." Salena took Fiora's shirt and slipped it on.

Fiora stepped out of the pant legs. "What do you mean, you won't hesitate again?"

The tight dress lacked both style and comfort. She had to jerk her body back and forth to shimmy into it.

"That night they killed our parents. I hesitated, and we were captured." Salena took a deep breath and finished putting on Fiora's clothing. "I'm so sorry. I will not hesitate again."

Fiora frowned at the memory. Thanks to Sten, it burned brightly in her mind. She'd relived it often, every painful detail. "You can't honestly blame your-self for that night." She tugged the hat off her head, and then the string binding her long hair. "We were children."

"Not according to Noire law." Salena's eyes hazed over as if she too recalled that night.

"We were children," Fiora repeated, not leaving room for argument. There was plenty of blame to go around about that night, and none of it landed on the three sisters. "Kneel."

Salena obeyed. Fiora brushed her fingers through her sister's hair to lift it away from her face. Before she finished, the door opened.

Her sister's husband poked his head in with his hand covering his eyes. "I heard your plan from outside. Are you dressed?"

Fiora wondered how he could have heard. They had not been talking very loudly.

"Yes, you can look," Salena said. "Do you have the ring?"

"Here." He held up the piece of jewelry.

"Show Fiora how to use it. You're going to escort her back to the party. I'll be out shortly." Salena paused long enough to kiss him.

Fiora averted her eyes at the affection, waiting until it was over. She then placed the cap on Salena's head. Her hands shook. She didn't like this idea. It was too big of a risk. "Don't forget to speak in riddles. I never tell them their futures plainly."

"I remember," Salena said, standing.

Fiora grabbed her sister's hands. There was so much she wanted to say. "I still cannot see my own destiny, so if this goes poorly, I love you, and thank you."

"Nothing is going to happen to you," Salena said. "Stay by Grier. You can trust him with your life."

Grier took Fiora's hand. At the contact, she felt the heat of flames erupting around them, and heard the crackling of a fire. He slid a ring onto her finger and released her. "Twist the setting when you're ready."

Fiora glanced at her hand and turned the stone. Pain erupted all over her body, and she felt as if something pushed from inside her to get out. The sensation didn't last long, and when it was over, she was staring at a body that was not her own.

"Go," Salena ordered.

"I still say—" The whine of her own voice caused Fiora to flinch.

"You'll get used to it," Salena told her, gently nudging her to leave.

Grier led her in awkward silence toward the banquet. He kept glancing over his shoulder toward his wife and then down at her.

"How long have you been married?" she asked.

"It's new," he answered, distracted. "I don't like this."

"Me either. Should we get Salena and switch back?" Fiora asked. He probably wanted his wife safe, more so than a sister-by-marriage stranger.

To her surprise, he answered, "No. I trust her, and I don't have a better plan. How else are we to get you out of here? I am of the understanding you cannot do what she does."

The words stung a little, though she wasn't sure why. Maybe it was the intimidating way he said them.

He again stared at her. His eyes shifted with an inner light, managing to be both mesmerizing and terrifying at the same time.

"I forgot how fascinated people seemed to be by seeing the three of us together," Fiora said.

Grier instantly averted his gaze, as if just now realizing he was staring. "You don't look like her now. Though, it is a remarkable resemblance before you put the ring on. Your hair is longer."

Fiora glanced at her strange hands. She slipped her morphed fingers onto his arm and let him lead her into the crowded hall. The timelines hit her with renewed force. She tried to steady her breath. The people did not turn to stare at her like before as they kept their attention on the small stage, awaiting her return. Well, that wasn't exactly true. A few of the nearby aliens seemed fascinated with her body. She glanced down, suddenly recognizing a weight on her chest. Those two jiggly spaceports were new. No wonder she'd felt like something had been trying to get out of her when she'd morphed. It had been planet Breast and her sister planet Boob.

"Is everything all right?" Grier asked in concern.

"These breasts are huge. It's like lugging around two docked spaceships," she blurted before biting the inside of her lip.

He arched a brow. More eyes turned to look at her.

"Sorry I can't lie. Please don't ask me any more questions," she pleaded in a whisper.

He nodded once.

Salena entered the hall, watching her feet as she walked. Fiora concentrated on breathing. Salena now looked like Salena...or rather, like Fiora.

Salena might be able to take her place on stage, but she couldn't take the timelines flowing into Fiora's thoughts from the crowd. Her temple throbbed.

"Who is next?"

At her sister's voice, she glanced up to find the Lykan man approaching Salena, now sitting in her chair.

"They are not supposed to do that," Fiora said in irritation, but there were no guards next to Salena to regulate the event. "Everyone gets one turn, one question."

She couldn't hear what the man asked Salena, but her sister stood from her chair and moved to whisper something in the Lykan's ear.

Grier stiffened next to her. His hand balled into a fist, and Fiora wondered if it was jealousy that fueled him. When she tried to look into his future, all she saw was flames and monsters.

Fiora's gaze moved over the floor to look at General Sten. He stared at Salena, probably noticing her lack of bodyguards.

"I hope my sister knows what she's doing," Fiora said as Salena retook her seat.

"I trust her," Grier answered.

No, it wasn't jealousy that fueled him. It was hidden within a tiny glimpse of his future, but she caught it.

"You do more than trust her," Fiora smiled, comforted somewhat to know that her sister would be in this man's future. That meant Salena would get out of here. "I can feel it between you two. You're connected. You have the kind of love for her that I have rarely seen in my life."

Grier gave a small laugh. "You are blunt like your sister. I take that to be a family trait."

"I do not believe I had to wait to go after a smelly Lykan," a Dokka trader announced. His words caused a round of laughter. The Lykan had been approaching a Slit'therne. He turned at the Dokka's comment.

Fiora's smile fell. The arguments were starting. Salena was pulling confessions from the crowd.

"And you with the lustful eyes?" Salena's voice lifted. "What are you thinking?"

"That I would like to bend over the Klennup's wife," another Dokka answered.

More laughter erupted.

Salena continued pulling the confessions from the crowd, turning them on each other.

"What is going on here?" General Sten demanded over the chaos.

"Dammit, Salena," Grier muttered as yelling turned to fighting. He grabbed Fiora's arm and navigated the crowd toward his wife. He kept his body angled to protect her from danger.

A slender man stumbled across their path. Grier nudged him out of the way. The gathering's timelines converged as their shared futures painted a clearer picture of the brawl that was about to happen.

Fiora saw the soldiers flooding the room seconds before it happened. She turned a high-pitched scream in their direction to get their attention. She pointed away from her sister. "Over there! The general!"

Since she couldn't lie and say the general needed help, it was as close as a diversion as she could manage.

The soldiers rammed their way through the crowd, knocking several of the guests over as they fought their way to their leader.

The timelines split apart, became as chaotic as the room, causing her head to spin. She didn't see a way out. There were too many soldiers, too many flying fists. Someone hit her shoulder and sent her stumbling. She felt dizzy and had to close her eyes. The emotion in the room was too much to sort through.

Fiora wasn't sure she would make it out of this mess alive. And so long as Salena was safe, she was all right with that outcome.

4

Movement caught Jaxx's attention, and he saw a uniformed soldier flying from the stronghold's door seconds before Grier burst through with two women in tow. The man landed on the ground and lay unconscious. Jaxx stretched his wings, ready to join any battle. As far as signs went, this wasn't subtle. The people below were oblivious to what happened on the clifftop.

Grier didn't hesitate as he ran, gripping each woman by a wrist, forcing them with him as he leaped off the side of the cliff. A faint scream sounded as they plummeted toward the ground. An outcropping blocked them from being seen by the people of Shelter City.

Jaxx flexed his wings, ready to surge from the watchtower rooftop. The women would not survive such a fall, but he trusted his cousin to protect them.

Before Jaxx could take flight, Grier transformed mid-fall and corrected his trajectory. Hands became talons. His wings flapped with force as he lifted the women into the safety of air. Though, knowing humans, Jaxx doubted they would be feeling too safe right now. Their legs kicked, and they both scrambled with their free hand to hold on to the talon wrapped around their wrists. Their bodies twisted against the dim sky as Grier dove, looping along the edge of the city as fast as he could fly. With any luck, no one would see what the crown prince was holding, at least not clearly, and it wasn't as if any of them could do anything to stop him.

Grier came to a jerking stop near the top of the watchtower and met Jaxx's gaze. Jaxx recognized Salena. She'd changed her clothes into a white tunic and pants. The other woman wore the morphing ring and looked as Salena had going into the facility.

Grier lowered the women gently to the earth.

Jaxx jumped off the tower to meet them. When his feet hit the ground, he shifted into his human form. Confining the size of the dragon into the body of a man was a painful process, but it didn't last long, and after decades he'd become used to it.

Jaxx ran to where the others had landed. Grier released the women before dropping to his feet next to them. He, too, shifted into his human form.

The morphed woman swayed on her feet, stumbling toward him. His vision shifted, taking in every movement as if it were imperative that he memorized the moment. The reaction was involuntary. Her green eyes met his briefly before she collapsed.

Jaxx caught the unconscious woman's limp body against his chest. A shiver of awareness worked over his naked form at the contact. Her dark auburn hair clung to his skin as he scooped his arm under her legs to lift her from the ground. He felt his body responding to the intimate press.

"I can't believe we did it." Salena made a weak noise as she held her stomach. She dropped to her knees next to Jaxx and looked at the woman in his arms.

"Wait..." Jaxx adjusted the unconscious woman as he tried to get Salena's attention. What was he supposed to do with her? His breathing deepened, and he tried to force his heartbeat to slow. "Salena...?"

Salena glanced at him, saying, "I'd like you to

meet my sister," as she reached to take the morphing ring off her sister's dangling hand.

The woman in his arms transformed as he held her. The auburn color of her hair lost some of its red. Her face thinned, the cheeks sinking as dark circles formed under her eyes. Her lips paled. She looked like Salena when Jaxx had first found her hiding in a cave near this very watchtower.

Salena had appeared just as ill-treated, weak, and had been starved near death. Anger boiled inside him. After seeing the rations the Cysgodians received, it was no surprise that the Federation starved their prisoners as a way to control them.

Things could not go on like this.

Before Jaxx could act on his growing rage, Grier said, "Jaxx, help me get them back to the dragon palace before Fiora regains consciousness. I'm afraid I gave her a terrifying ride."

Jaxx nodded and lowered Fiora gently to the ground. Something about her stirred the protective instincts in him, but he dismissed the deep emotions. Of course, he felt sorry for her and wanted to protect her. One look at her and he could see her human frailty. He didn't allow himself to read anything more into his feelings.

This was not the first time he'd be acting on the

edge of the law. It wasn't even the first time he'd flown through the sky with an unconscious woman clutched in his talons. There was no reason to feel this moment was special.

Jaxx let his dragon form take over his body before grabbing her by the shoulders and taking to the sky.

5

TIME LOST ALL MEANING WHEN THE FUTURE converged on the present.

The second Fiora was pulled out of the Federation facility by her brother-by-marriage, the yelling had started. It was as if thousands of people desperately tried to tell her their stories all at once. Their timelines pressed in on her, choking her as if she gasped to breathe from under a mountain of bodies. Ghostlike images appeared all around her. She'd barely had time to process the information before Grier had forced her to jump off the side of a cliff. She'd screamed out of fear, out of the need to get the yelling to stop, out of frustration when she didn't splatter against the ground.

But then Grier's hand around her wrist had changed into that of a beast, and she was yanked away from the promise of reprieve into a tumultuous flight through a green sky. Her body dangled over images of explosions and fires, and she undulated in the cold air like a flag, legs twisting behind her. Just like with her visions, her body had no control over what happened.

Why wouldn't they all just let the torment end?

Nothingness seemed like a nice alternative to the current images of explosions and the echoing screams of people dying that were now filling her thoughts.

For the brief second when they'd been falling, she felt relief that there was a ground that would stop everything. Blessed, permanent rest.

Silence.

Forever.

Fiora had the vague impression of touching down on firm earth before the vision of a naked man emerged from beside a watchtower. She didn't recognize him or the markings on his chest but felt as if his energy pulled her. Her legs wobbled as she felt herself stumbling toward him. Pain exploded behind her eyes. There were too many timelines, too many deaths in the valley settlement. The man's eyes were fire in the darkness. Death himself, perhaps, come to feast on the misery emanating from below. Panic had overwhelmed her senses, and she wanted the nothingness to take her.

But the dreams would only let the darkness win for so long. They started with a vengeance, trapping her in a weightless trance as she was forced to watch the end of a world. Nothing made sense. Explosions turned to desolate landscapes. Screams faded into hungry whimpers. Those who loved each other learned to hate as the world beyond chipped away all hope. The timelines were out of sequence, the pieces not fitting together. They came from too many voices, too many points of view.

People died. Spirits reversed in time to live. A hollow laugh echoed over a cry.

It was too much.

It needed to stop.

It would never stop.

Fiora wanted to tear out her eyes, but that wouldn't help. She wanted to deafen her ears, but the cries would remain in her brain.

She felt her body suspended in the air as if she flew without wings. Nausea built, reminding her of what it felt like during a spaceship's turbulent landing.

It never stopped.

Being a prisoner made to perform for the Federation was hardly a dream scenario. Still, at least in prison she'd been locked away from the tragedy of the outside world. She could hide under a blanket and beg the guards to leave if the visions became too loud.

Here, from the sky, she saw smoke rising from the scorched earth. But it wasn't real. She wasn't awake. She couldn't fly. This wasn't her future sequence she was trapped in. None of it made sense.

It never stopped.

Fiora felt herself being led into the side of a mountain. Sometimes the visions made little sense. People did not walk through stone. Or maybe this was the future of an elemental. Inside the mountain was a palace with polished red walls and floors.

Why wouldn't it stop?

Just a small break, that was all she needed. A sharp pain shot through the back of her eye. This headache was going to be a bad one.

Murmured voices came from hidden alcoves as she shuffled through a hallway. At least now she was on her feet. Someone pulled her hand, leading her past stone pedestals. She kept her eyes down, using what little concentration she could muster to keep from throwing up on the clean floor.

"This way," a gruff voice commanded, jerking her around a corner. She almost crashed into the wall but managed to lift her hand to block the impact.

Fiora finally glanced up to see where they were going and instantly regretted it. Death strode naked before her, tugging her through a lavish hall. Statues of fearsome beasts were set in alcoves on each side. Tapestries and paintings decorated the walls. They depicted horrible battle scenes between two very different kinds of humanoid creatures.

They turned another corner, entering a hallway much like the one they'd just left. She wished for darkness so that she may hide. Monsters couldn't see her in the dark. If they couldn't see her, they couldn't get her. Not like in the light. That's what her mother had told them.

Her mind had been overloaded with strong visions, and it became difficult to decipher if this was a delusion, the future, or really happening. The warmth from Death's hand rolled up her chilled arm, a palpable wave that forced her to pay attention to the sensation. Even as she feared him, she clung to that hint of reality.

The images of destruction began to ease as he pulled her around another corner. The yells became quiet echoes. Fiora found herself staring at the muscles beneath his skin as they moved in an undulating manner beneath the surface. Mesmerized, she focused on his back. Each tiny movement became a separate entity worthy of study.

The warmth continued up her arm. They turned yet another corner. His bare feet made soft sounds on the hard floor.

Her heartbeat began to slow, dislodging the pressure in her throat. She took a deep breath. The ragged sound must have caught the man's attention because he stopped walking and turned to look at her.

Green eyes met hers, filled with concern. This was not Death. This was a man—a *naked* man.

"You do not look well," he stated. "Do you require a medic or food?"

Fiora pulled her hand away from him and looked around the hallway. She couldn't decipher how exactly she'd made it into the building. Walking through the side of a mountain didn't seem logical unless it was some kind of barrier wall mirage.

"...have children. I so want to be a grandmother. I miss my dragon babies..."

The excited words echoed from the distance. Apparently, the voices weren't going to stop either.

"Don't look at me, son," a man said with laughter in his voice. *"I will never temper my wife's pleasure."*

"When are we?" Fiora whispered, confused. Death didn't answer.

Fiora noticed that light came from decorative holes above, but there were no windows. The red walls and floors appeared seamlessly cut, rather than constructed. Her eyes went to the sculpture of a beast wearing a crown. Though the expression was not fierce, that didn't stop the creature from looking like the thing from which nightmares were born.

"Mother, let me take Salena home."

Fiora recognized the voice. The sound felt more from the present. It was that of her sister's husband. Maybe these weren't visions.

Salena. Salena was alive and safe.

Fiora swayed on her feet. The man grabbed her by the upper arm and pulled her closer to him. She frowned at his familiar handling. Her body stung, and the contact was painful even though he didn't try to harm her.

"Unhand me," she whispered. The sound came out harsh, even though that wasn't her intention. Her voice was trapped in her throat.

He instantly released her.

Fiora swayed again. She couldn't be touched.

Not right now. Too many emotions had bombarded her body, and her skin burned as if her nerves had been sheered raw. At times like this, she could barely remember her own name.

"Welcome to the family, Lady Salena."

Salena. She needed to find her sister.

The cheery woman's loud voice drew Fiora's attention. She couldn't see the woman who spoke, but she knew that the queen of the dragon people was talking to her sister. The more immediate impressions forced themselves into her mind. Salena and her mother-by-marriage would have an awkward start but would eventually settle into a relationship of mutual respect.

It never stopped.

"I can't keep doing this," Fiora whispered.

"What do you mean?" the man next to her asked.

Fiora rubbed her temple as she glanced sideways at him. She hated that she was unable to tell a lie. "I want to die. It never stops."

He did not appear pleased with her honesty. "What never stops?"

"I'm tired of living with this—"

"Let me know if there is anything I can bring you," the queen shouted enthusiastically. The sound of footsteps came from the same direction.

Fiora was grateful for the interruption. When she started to lift her hand in a silent plea to stop him from continuing the conversation, a wave of awareness came over her. She turned more fully toward him. She'd been confused before when all the death and destruction hit her, but she felt the man's future clearly now. No wonder she was sick to her stomach when she was around him.

"Why are you looking at me like that?" he asked, frowning.

"I'm so sorry." Fiora hated that she was compelled to answer honestly. Tears brimmed her eyes. When she looked at him, all she saw was emptiness. That is why she'd confused him for Death. He wasn't Death. He was destined to die. "You have a death mark."

The man stiffened. Could she blame him?

Fiora had learned very quickly as a young girl that people didn't necessarily want the truth. They said they did. They said they wanted to know the future, but it wasn't true. They wanted her to tell them the future they wanted to hear, not what really would come to pass.

Could she blame them? When the futures of so many were about to be cut short? Why would they want to hear how painful the end would be?

It never stopped.

Grier escorted Salena toward them. Her sister's hair was a tangled mess, and she wore Fiora's white tunic. Grier was covered in clumps of dried mud. The disguise had been somewhat more convincing when he'd arrived at the facility, but now he looked like he'd been traveling for days without access to a decontaminator.

Salena approached, only to stop near the monster statue. She leaned against it, taking a deep breath as she clung to a stone shoulder.

Grier appeared concerned. "Salena?"

"Move me and I'm throwing up on one of you, Grier," Salena answered. "I need the world to stop spinning first."

Fiora tried to keep her head from whirling. She pressed her hands to her forehead. The marked man touched her arm gently to turn her toward him. She was sure he meant well, but the slight jolt of her body sent a shockwave through her, and she ended up heaving a stomach full of nutrient paste onto the man's crotch.

He jerked his hand back.

Fiora covered her mouth, mortified by what she'd done. The man stood frozen with his hands to his sides as if he wasn't sure what to do about the mess. When she opened her mouth to apologize, another wave of nausea hit her, and she covered her lips in an attempt to stop a repeat performance. She swayed slightly on her feet.

"Let's get you ladies someplace where you can rest." Grier motioned that Fiora should walk with Salena away from the statue.

Fiora sidestepped the mess, glancing up at the marked man in apology. Salena stayed close to her side.

"Jaxx, Kane should be home," Grier said. "You can bathe there. He'll have something you can wear. And call a servant to send a cleaning droid to help with this, please."

Jaxx. The marked man had a name.

Fiora took hold of her sister's arm, leaning into Salena for support. All she wanted was to get away from everyone.

"I promise you'll be safe here," Grier said. It took her a moment to realize he spoke to her. "No one can get to you while you are in the palace."

"They'll come," Fiora whispered. Even though he didn't ask the question, she felt compelled to warn him. At least he'd be able to keep Salena safe. That's the best she could hope for. "It won't take them long to figure it out who took us. Two beasts in the sky will not go unnoticed."

"They're called dragons," Salena corrected.

"You have many fights ahead." Fiora needed them to understand what she'd seen, even as she didn't understand it all herself. "I see red and violet—"

"Shh, you don't have to speak now." Salena shushed her as she patted her back. "You don't have to look at the future. We're safe now."

Grier went ahead of them to open a thick wooden door and then waited for them to enter before him.

Fiora paused before stepping through the door. Her mind was a jumbled mess. "Two is stronger." She grabbed her sister's hand and held tight. "Together, we might be able to find our missing piece."

Piera. They still needed to find Piera. She couldn't forget. Her head filled with so many time-lines that it would be easy to lose herself.

"Do you know anything?" Fiora insisted.

"No, and I've searched many places." Salena guided her into a home.

Fiora saw a circular couch and walked toward it. Her mouth tasted awful. Her stomach churned. She sat hard against the cushions, tipping to her side while her feet were still on the floor. It wasn't comfortable, but she didn't care.

Let the darkness come.

For the love of everything, please let the darkness take me.

6

"WHAT IS THAT SMELL?" KANE FLINCHED AS HE held open the door to his home. He glanced over his cousin and automatically started to close his door without inviting him inside.

Several members of the Draig royal family lived in the mountain palace. The front was carved so that it blended into the side of the mountain, hiding it from above. Well, at least that was the original intent. The small village and surrounding valley with worn paths leading to the palace gave away the location, as did the barracks and training yard along the side.

Inside the mountain, there was plenty of space for expansion. If Jaxx wanted, he could've had apartments in the palace like his cousins. Like his father, Prince Yusef, Jaxx much preferred to live in the forest surrounded by the ancient trees bigger than his home.

Jaxx placed his hand on the door and grumbled, "I need to borrow some clothes."

Kane let him push the door open with a small laugh. "Not before you bathe." He glanced down and grimaced. "Is that—?"

"You need to have a cleaning droid sent to the hall near Grier's dragon statue," Jaxx said.

"A droid? What by all the gods is going on?" Kane still seemed more amused than alarmed. "Is there a celebration someone forgot to invite me to?"

"Hardly," Jaxx grumbled, forcing his way inside.

Kane had been training to take over his father's position as the royal Draig ambassador, so it made sense that he lived in the palace. The home looked like many of the others. Light came from a series of tubes inside the ceiling, shining through holes. The open space had a couch around a firepit. There was a food simulator next to a table, although most of the palace meals were taken in the main hall as a group. Tapestries depicting scenes from the past hung on the wall next to banners. The palace hadn't changed much since they were children.

"What are you staring at?" Kane asked, his tone

more concerned than before. "Seriously, Jaxx, you're starting to worry me."

Jaxx realized he'd been staring at a tapestry depicting a battle between the Draig and Var. "Do you ever think about how much simpler it was back then? When we only had to fight each other and not the rest of the universe?"

"The Federation is hardly the rest of the universe," Kane dismissed. "And if you tell me you're longing for the old cat-shifter wars, I'm going to say you've been spending too much time with Grace. She was just asking me about some old law she found to dissolve her marriage treaty."

"She doesn't want to dissolve the treaty to go back to war. She wants the freedom to choose who she marries," Jaxx defended his cousin. He'd always felt bad for her. Grace had been born into a treaty between the cats and dragons. As far as the planet was concerned, her destiny was to unite the two kingdoms. The betrothal was a symbol of unity that had helped sustain peace their entire lives. It went against everything dragon-shifters believed in when it came to finding mates.

On the day each dragon child was born their fathers went to a lake, dove beneath the surface, and mined a crystal from the bottom. The dragon children then wore these crystals until the day it started to glow. This is how the gods communicated with them. When the crystal glowed, that meant they had found their mate. It was never wrong.

Prince Zoran and Princess Pia, Grace's parents, had not intended for the betrothal to stand for so many years. None of the elders had. In fact, because female shifter births were so rare, none of them thought they'd have to go through with a marriage. The proposed betrothment was to be symbolic, a show that both sides were willing to make peace. What the elders hadn't counted on was the romanticized view that had taken hold amongst the people when Grace was born.

Grace's crystal had been a torment to her. It represented a path she was not supposed to take—one to true love and happiness. In that, she was alone. Jaxx had made a pact with his cousin. He'd hid her crystal, and she'd hid his. On the day she was freed from her betrothal would be the day they returned the stones. As long as she was held from her future, he would wait for his. That way she was not alone.

That had been years ago.

Jaxx moved toward the decontaminator room to clean up, knowing his cousin wouldn't follow him inside. He ignored the water bath that drew from the hot springs in the mountain and always bubbled at a pleasant temperature. Instead, he stepped into a decontaminator and let the lasers efficiently clean him. He closed his eyes as the lights danced over his naked body.

Why was he thinking about his crystal? Unless his mother brought up her wish to see him married, he rarely thought about the stone.

Fiora.

There was something special about her. He'd felt it the second she'd landed in his arms. Maybe before that. It wasn't attraction—not to her morphed body, anyway. And it would be strange to say he was attracted to her when he hadn't been attracted to her sister, Salena. They looked fairly identical.

Still, even now, he could feel the awareness of her in his arms.

Was it merely circumstances that made him think so?

Jaxx had a death mark. It didn't take much imagination to deduce what that probably meant. Was the knowledge causing his mind to toss out regrets? He had no wife, no children. He had never been in love.

He had no reason to mistrust the woman when she said he was death marked. He had already witnessed Salena's power to force the truth out of people. It stood to reason Fiora's abilities would be just as strong.

Fiora's gaze had been so apologetic and sad when she'd looked at him. He wondered what details she saw but was too afraid to ask. No one wanted to hear how or when they were going to die, him included.

Death.

The woman's face haunted him. Those eyes, so sad, so troubled.

In the abstract, he'd always been ready for death. If he died fighting for the people of Shelter City, or for his fellow shifters, so be it. He wasn't afraid of fate.

Yet, part of the appeal had always been the not knowing. Each time he snuck into Shelter City, or smuggled decontaminators, he did so with the belief that he would come out alive. Hope was a great thing.

But take that hope away, only to replace it with certainty? That only left death.

The laser decontaminator had finished by the time he came back from his thoughts. His vision focused. Jaxx wasn't sure how long he'd been standing in the inactive unit.

He stepped out of the decontaminator and went

to the living room. Kane shoved clothes at his chest as Jaxx walked out the door.

"I ordered a cleaning droid sent to the statue," Kane said.

Jaxx nodded. He dropped a tunic shirt on the floor and pulled on the pair of loose pants. Then, leaning over, he swiped the shirt from the floor. He held it in his fist.

"Can I stay here?" Jaxx asked.

"You never have to ask, cousin," Kane said. "All that I have is yours. Except for my bed."

Jaxx nodded.

Kane moved to his table. Parchment was piled neatly into five stacks next to an electronic clipboard. "Hungry?"

"No." Jaxx couldn't think of eating when his mind was full. He sat across from his cousin. He pulled a stack of documents toward him and read, "Syog negotiation guidelines. What are we negotiating?"

"Nothing, ever, if I can help it." Kane leaned forward and put his finger on the second paragraph.

Jaxx read, "Each negotiator will be allowed three strikes upon the other's man..." He lifted his head and grimaced. "They negotiate by kicking each other in the manhood?" He slowly shook his head. "And you *want* to be an ambassador?"

Kane gave a wry laugh. "The day those aliens come to visit might be the day I join you hiding in the forest."

"I'm hardly hiding," Jaxx grumbled. He gestured at the papers. "What is all this anyway?"

"I'm rescanning documents that were lost when the palace databases went down." Kane crossed his arms over his chest. "It's as thrilling as it sounds."

Jaxx's eyes went to his cousin's wrist. Kane's crystal was sewn into place on the leather band.

"What happened?" Kane asked.

"I'll tell you later." Jaxx pried his eyes away from Kane's dormant mating crystal. He pushed up from the table and moved to rest on the couch. "I need to sleep."

It was a lame excuse, but it was the only thing he could think of to avoid Kane's direct questions. He wasn't ready to talk about the death mark.

As he lay down, hiding his face from his cousin's view, his thoughts turned to Fiora and the struggle in her eyes. They stirred an ache deep inside him. He wanted to find her and protect her.

The impulse might prove necessary soon enough. The Federation would know that she was missing, and they'd come looking. Maybe that is how he died. Perhaps it was his fate to protect her from going back.

"Jaxx?" Kane's voice was insistent.

Jaxx didn't open his eyes as he gave a monosyllabic moan in response.

"I'll bring you a tray back from the dining hall," he said. The sound of the door opening and closing followed the words.

7

ALL AROUND HER WAS THE LINGERING nightmare of death. The hollowness of it stayed inside her.

Fiora should have been happy to see her sister, and yet, how could she enjoy the reunion with the predictions peeking at her through her peripheral vision?

Flames came from the sky. Explosions lit Shelter City. Screams echoed on repeat in her head. The world was on fire, and she could do nothing about it. Well, she could pray no one would ask her a question that made her tell of the upcoming events. Not knowing was better than an entire planet huddling in fear and begging her to find answers.

Fiora felt a tickle and wiped the back of her hand

across her nose. Blood smeared her skin. It reminded her of the prison walls splattered in red. The guards should have let her die.

Even with a nosebleed, things felt calmer now that she was in a guest suite, away from people. Her sister had arranged the new accommodations. The walls were the same red stone as the rest of the palace she'd seen. Tapestries covered the walls, the woven cloths depicting landscapes from what she guessed were parts of the planet, since she'd only seen the inside of the facility and fragments from other people's futures.

Salena would never say it, but Fiora knew she had frightened her sister with talk of upcoming death. She didn't want to tell her, but Salena kept asking how she was and Fiora was compelled to answer in detail.

The images in her head were like residual imprints that would grow less insistent in time if she didn't go back to Shelter City. Today, they were being replaced by visions of an encounter outside the mountain palace of the monster people.

Draig palace. Dragons. Not monsters. They were men who shifted into dragons or dragons who shifted into men.

And flew.

Fiora touched her stomach, remembering the flight all too well. If she never took to the air again, it would be too soon.

Thinking of the sky moved her mind to Jaxx. A strange tranquility came over her when she thought of him. Maybe because he didn't have a future. She felt terrible about his fate, but not seeing his tomorrows meant she could consider him without pain. He had such a steadying presence.

Steadying? Who was she kidding? Sexy. He had a *sexy* presence.

She'd gotten a pretty good view as he'd led her naked through the halls of the palace. Windblown dark hair and brooding eyes created the perfect balance of man and beast. Within the body of the man, she sensed the animal—caged energy that flowed beneath the surface of his skin.

When he had been in the form of a dragon, she'd sensed his humanity. The beast had been gentle with her when they'd landed.

The guest suite was smaller than her sister's home, but compared to her prison cell, it was a mansion. The ample space made her feel incredibly small. The high ceilings and walls covered in imposing tapestries gave the illusion that she was a child in the land of giants. A massive, winged beast—

blast it all, dragon—a massive, winged *dragon* was depicted in thread with fire shooting from a fang-filled mouth.

Foolish as it was, she found herself avoiding eye contact with the material creature.

A light tap sounded. Fiora sat up on the couch and tilted her head to listen in the silence.

Tap-tap.

She turned her attention to the door. The tap turned into a louder knock. She frowned, not wanting anyone to come near her.

Guilt instantly assaulted her at the notion of ignoring whoever sought her attention. She was a guest. They kept her safe from the Federation. Without them, she'd be eating nutrient paste and staring at sterilized walls.

Fiora stood and moved slowly toward the door, ready to push out any images that tried to reveal themselves to her. A feeling of calm came through the wood as she touched the handle.

Jaxx.

Fiora pulled open the door. Jaxx's back was to her, and he was walking away. He wore a tunic shirt, tight pants, and boots. Her mind automatically offered to compare the image of him in clothing to the one of him naked.

"Yes?" she asked, her voice not as strong as she would have liked. "Jaxx?"

He turned, and the depth of his green eyes struck a chord in her.

"Did you need me for something?" she asked.

He hesitated before coming closer to her. "I thought maybe you were resting. I hope I'm not disturbing you. I can come back later."

Fiora shook her head. Again, she didn't pick up much from his future. She saw him walking through a door, but the impression was light. "Not really. I was sitting and enjoying the silence."

"I understand." He nodded once and started to back away. "I will leave you to your contemplation. I have no wish to interrupt."

"You're not interrupting. Your timeline is quiet. It doesn't add to my headache." Fiora saw the slight flinch when she implied his death mark. There was nothing she could do about it, or her compulsion to speak the truth at all times. "Did you come to ask me about your future?"

To her surprise, he said, "No. I came to tell you about yours."

"Oh?" Fiora wasn't sure what to say to that. "Can you...? Are you like...me?"

At that, he gave a small smile. It was a subtle shift

of his mouth, but there was a playfulness to it she didn't expect. "I have a feeling there has never been a woman like you, Lady Fiora."

"Just Fiora. I'm not a lady," she corrected.

"All women are ladies here," he countered. "Especially the sister of our future queen. If anyone dares to imply otherwise, they will have to answer to a kingdom of dragons."

She waited to see if he would laugh, but he didn't. She felt the truth in his words. There was honor in this place. She saw it in Grier and his love for her sister. She felt it in the guards who had walked past hours before. She detected it in the queen when she'd met Salena for the first time.

"May I visit with you a moment?" he asked.

"Of course." Fiora gestured that he should come inside. "You have more right to be here than I do. I'm only a refugee living on the good graces of my sister and her husband."

"I don't believe that's true. You're part of the Draig royal family now," Jaxx answered.

The certainty of his words struck her. It had been a long time since she had been part of a family of any kind. Until Salena appeared in the stronghold, she'd convinced herself that her sisters were both dead, and she was the only one left.

"This palace is your home, more so than mine. I choose to live in the forest," he continued.

"The forest sounds nicer than a palace," she answered, jealous of the idea. "Fewer people. I miss living in the forest with my family on Noire."

He gestured toward her face. "The visions take much out of you. I can't imagine what that must be like. Do you need a personal medic?"

She touched her nose. It no longer bled, but a smear of evidence might have remained.

As if deciding his own answer, he said, "I will have a device sent to you. It will be yours to keep."

"This nosebleed is not new," she assured him. "There is little a medic device can do. At best it can force me to sleep until the headache goes away."

They stood facing each other. Without the onslaught of his future, it became both comforting and strange to have a conversation. Her own thoughts were not crowded out of her mind. She could appreciate the depth in his gaze, the shape of his mouth, the width of his shoulders. A tremor of awareness wiggled through her. There was plenty to be attracted to.

She'd seen him walking naked through the halls. The image came back in vivid colors. It seemed strange that a giant beast could fit inside such a perfect body. Time seemed to slow down when she looked at him. The future stopped as if its transmission was paused.

"Is there anything that can relieve the discomfort of your visions?" He looked like he genuinely wanted to help her.

"Chandoo or death," she answered.

Blast her constant honesty.

His expression was about what she'd expect when asking a member of the royal family to buy illegal drugs for her. His eyes narrowed at the suggestions, and he gave a firm shake of his head. "I'm sorry. I can't help you with those."

"I assumed as much." She slowly walked toward the couch to put distance between them. The directness of his intent gaze caused her heart to beat a little faster than usual. Her thoughts raced, but not like before. Now they collided with her impressions and needs. Only she wasn't sure what to think. "I want to apologize for vomiting on you. Between the visions and the flight, I am afraid I was not in control of my stomach."

"Think no more of it," Jaxx assured her. He followed her, slowly making his way toward the couch. His eyes didn't leave her. "I apologize for the rough flight."

"You helped save me from the Federation. I'm in your debt for that." Fiora remained standing, unsure of what to do. Generally, by this point in a conversation, she was concerned with keeping images out of her head. With Jaxx, the emptiness of his future let her have her own thoughts. Too bad she still couldn't figure out what those should be.

"That is why I have come." Jaxx shifted his weight, and she found herself mimicking his pose. "I wanted to let you know that General Sten has relinquished his claim on you. There is no reason for you to fear him. You are safe."

Safe. What an odd word. As long as she was breathing, she would never be safe. Her curse would always be a threat. There would always be those who would like to know what she could see.

"I assumed as much, but it is good to hear he relinquished his claim and has gone away for now," she said. "But you are wrong to say I should not fear him."

"You assumed?"

"I had visions of the queen scaring him more than the dragons, and his soldiers leaving." Fiora was proud of herself for calling him a dragon and not a monster. She closed her eyes, trying to isolate the vision out of the many swimming in her head.

Repeating the queen's words, heard by a soldier watching the interplay that happened at the palace entryway, she said, "*Any off-world prisoner brought to or captured on this planet by visiting authority, that would be the Federation, must be divulged to the royal shifter families, that would be us, immediately. Since we have not received such documentation of...*" She paused, trying to grasp at the string of thought as the timeline merged with that of the king. "*I can only assume that this is a misunderstanding. Otherwise, you are in violation of the temporary settlement agreement and must at once vacate this planet. Of course, we would welcome those who wish to remain in the settlement known as Shelter City to stay, with the understanding that they were no longer under Federation rule, but free to choose whether or not they wish to leave or become true Qurilixen citizens. We would welcome them with open hearts.*"

Fiora opened her eyes, wondering if this was the moment that brought forth the end of Shelter City. The dragons would have thought it a moment of victory, but the general was not a man to take the actions lightly. He was a man of control, and the dragons had taken away his psychic toy.

Was the imminent destruction because they'd saved her?

"That is exactly what the queen told General Sten. I would swear it was word for word, or at least very close," he said.

"It was word for word," she assured him. "It was brave of her to try."

"I think she rather enjoyed telling the general off. I know we all enjoyed watching her do it." Jaxx gave a small laugh.

Fiora tried to return his smile but couldn't.

"I'm trying to keep in mind that you don't want to be asked questions," Jaxx said, "but I have them."

"You want to know about your death," Fiora concluded. "I'm sorry I told you. I don't like giving that news."

"No." He shook his head firmly. "No man should ever know when the end is coming. I don't blame you for telling me. I know you can't help it. But I don't wish to know more. I can't let fear dictate my actions. I must go on as I am meant to."

On that she agreed with him, but the comment still took her by surprise. "Then what is your question?"

His eyes fixed on hers. "Do you want to be here?"

Want.

That one word echoed in her mind. Did she *want*?

"No." The truth came out of her before she even realized what the truth would be.

He slowly nodded. "Do you want to be taken back to the facility?"

"No." She shook her head.

"What do you want?" he asked.

A tear slipped down her cheek. "To travel back in time, to the day before my parents were killed and my sisters were taken from me. I want to know that love and acceptance again. I want to sleep without fear. I want to be away from all the timelines. Every single one of them ends in death because that is where life leads. Death. There's so much of it here. I hear the distant screams. I sense them like nails scratching against my skin, clawing and begging me for help. There is nothing I can do but watch it replay from every angle."

"Screaming?" He closed some of the distance between them. "Here? In the palace?"

"Shelter City," she said. "I saw its end, and it is not pleasant. There will be an explosion. Everything will set on fire." Fiora shivered and rubbed her arms. "They can't escape it. There all this desperation and fear. It will feed on everyone, building and churning and erupting."

"Did you see what triggered it?" he asked.

A tear slipped down her cheek. "Please don't ask me to try. There's so much. So many reasons. So many thoughts."

She felt a tickle under her nose and wiped at the fresh blood.

His mouth opened, and she could see he was torn.

Fiora wished she could be deceitful. Then she could trick him into escorting her back to the Federation base. One quick flight, and he could drop her off at the facility door. She'd walk right back into captivity. Instead, all she had was the truth, which was uncertain and shaky.

"I think I know what might change it," she said. "If you take me back to the Federation and give me to the general, we might stop this future from happening. Or we might not. The visions flooded me when I left the facility. Salena's coming for me shifted the future. This might undo it."

"So, the future is not set?" he asked. She heard the hope in his words.

"It's fluid and churning. By the time it reaches me, it's usually set on its course, and it takes a great feat to interfere with its flow." The screams tried to get louder, and she had to concentrate on forcing them away. She again swiped at her nose.

"If I say I'll take you back, can't you look to see if that will change things?" He lifted his hand as if he would catch her as she swayed on her feet. He didn't touch her.

"I won't know until I actually go. I usually can't see my direct future, even in someone else's timeline. Ironic, right?" She gave a humorless laugh. "A psychic who can't even predict what she's going to have for dinner unless it's green nutrient paste in the Federation stronghold, but that's less of a prediction and just the only thing they fed me."

He glanced over her body, his gaze lingering on her waist. "Now that we know there is an immediate threat, we will figure out another way. You should not have to go back."

"The universe does not run on should."

Jaxx's eyes moved back to capture hers. His steady gaze did something to her. The calmness she felt in him gave her strength. His presence didn't invoke visions. His nearness seemed to cast away the emotions scratching at her skin.

"I should never have been brought to this planet in the first place. I should not have had my family ripped from me." She found herself inching closer to him and forced her feet to stop and hold their place. "I should not have been born with this curse."

Fiora frowned and looked down at her hands.

"I am dwelling in sorrow when I know there is much worse that can happen." She needed to stop feeling sorry for herself. Fiora wasn't used to so much space in her head. "It's like you're too quiet, and now I'm circling in my own thoughts. And since I can't see your future, I'm just babbling. And I know I'm doing it, but I can't compel myself to—"

Jaxx placed his hands on her shoulders.

"Stop," she finished with a deep inhale.

Warmth spread down her arms, and everything became still. The echoes of distant screams silenced completely. All dread dissipated.

He let her go and took a step back. The murmur of her promotions instantly flooded back.

She reached for him, placing her hand on his shirt. It didn't work like anticipated, and she slid her palm up to press to his bare neck. The sounds again stopped. She tried with her opposite hand on his cheek. The same reaction happened.

Fiora stared at the contact. She released him, and the visions came back. She touched him, and they left. She released him and then touched him, over and over, testing the results. The connection turned the feelings on and off like a switch.

"What are you?" she whispered, her hands on his face.

"A dragon-shifter," he answered, confused. "A Draig prince. My father is a prince and brother of the king. My grandmother wanted all of her grandchildren to have the royal titles, not just Grier and his brothers."

"What is this?" she insisted, staring at where her hands cupped his face.

"Uh...?" He didn't pull free of her hold. "It is my face."

Her thumb moved closer to his lips as he spoke. In the calm, she shifted her focus from inside her head to the feel of his skin, and the shadow of a beard that had started to grow. Heat radiated down her arms. Her headache lessened.

"I don't want to release you," she whispered.

"I don't want you to," he said.

"There is silence in you." She worked her fingers against his cheeks, not breaking contact. "I've never seen this before."

He mimicked her actions, cupping her face. The contact startled her, and she reached to cover his hands with hers. She felt his wrist. The intimate touch of him holding her caused a shiver to work its way over her, and she slowly pulled his hands away.

"I'm sorry. I should not have overstepped." She didn't want to release him. "Please pass the appropriate apologies to your wife."

"Wife?" Jaxx arched a brow.

She reluctantly released him, and the undercurrent of screams returned, more noticeable now that she'd gone without hearing them.

Fiora gestured at his wrist. "My sister told me about your customs. She said that the unmated men wore crystals on their wrists or necks to signify their status. I have seen them on some of the people here. You do not have one."

"I do not have a wife," he said.

"Oh, I'm sorry. When did you lose her?" Fiora asked.

"There is no her," he explained.

"My apologies. Him. When did you lose him?" she asked.

"There is no him."

"Then...?" She wasn't sure what to say.

"I am not mated. I simply choose not to wear my crystal. It's a long and complicated story."

"But then how will your dragon know if you are to be mated?" Fiora asked. "I know my sister was only telling me about local culture to take my mind from my premonitions, but I admit, I find the whole concept of glowing crystals to be fascinating. Do you really choose who you are to be with by using a stone? How does that work?"

Jaxx nodded. "Yes. That is how our marriages are decided. It is an old tradition, but one that never fails us. It is simple. A crystal glows when we are next to our potential mate. It's said to be an amplification of what we already know."

"But you don't wish to be married?" she asked.

"Of course I..." He lowered his gaze. "I'm not sure what I want matters."

"Because of the death mark," she concluded. Fiora sighed. "I'm sorry. I hate myself sometimes. I don't want to say these things. I just can't stop them."

"You do not need to keep apologizing to me," he said. "I understand that you cannot temper your words. I find it refreshing."

"Refreshing." At that, she gave a surprised laugh. "I don't think anyone has ever called my conversation refreshing."

"You appear exhausted. Is there anything I can do to make your stay here easier?" Jaxx looked as if he wanted to stay even as he moved toward the door.

"Don't leave," she blurted.

"You wish for my company?"

"Yes. Actually, you're right. I'm exhausted."

"So, you do *not* wish for my company?"

"I wish for you to let me touch you while I sleep. Something about your skin calms the visions, and it's so quiet. I think, maybe, if you were here, I might not have the nightmares." Fiora bit her lip. "I know it's a strange request, and it takes advantage of your generosity. I apologize."

"Stop apologizing," he admonished. "I am happy to remain as your guard while you sleep."

"Really?" She let loose a deep and trembling breath. "Thank you." Fiora glanced around. "Should we...?" She looked toward the bed and then decided on the couch. She gestured toward the cushions.

Jaxx nodded. He sat on the end of the couch and arranged a pillow next to his hip. "Come."

Fiora lay on the couch, facing the back. The top of her head was close to his thigh. He dropped his arm to hold her hand lightly.

The screams stopped, and she breathed a sigh of relief as she closed her eyes. "You're better than Chandoo."

8

WELL, THIS WAS AWKWARD.

Jaxx watched over Fiora as she slept. Of course, his body wanted to do much more than watch, and the arousal pressing against his pants refused to ease. When had he turned into a complete dragon who could not control his base urges? This woman needed protection, and all he could think about was not glancing at the soft rise and fall of her chest.

Which he was doing. Again.

Blast it all!

There was a difference between lying and choosing not to speak. Neither of which seemed to be options for Fiora. He couldn't imagine being compelled to say every thought in his head. If he had, he would have confessed his attraction to her at a time when she was talking about the destruction of a city.

Not his proudest moment.

Fiora looked just like her sister, but he didn't see Salena when he looked at her. He saw someone who'd had a rougher road to travel—and when he'd found Salena, she'd been starved and dying in a cliffside cave near Shelter City, so that was saying something.

He'd thought Queen Rigan standing up to the general was amusing at the time, but with Fiora's warning, all humor faded. She was right. He didn't have to be psychic to predict the general would retaliate. He was the type of man who always wanted retribution, even if it wasn't justified.

Jaxx released Fiora's hand to stretch his arms over his head. Instantly, she gave a small moan and turned on the couch. Her forehead wrinkled with a deep frown, and she began to toss in her sleep.

"Those poor babies," she mumbled.

"Hey, easy," he soothed as he dropped his arms to make contact with her skin. He took her hand in his. She instantly calmed. Her fingers twitched against him.

After several moments, he pulled his hand away, letting it hover over her. She moaned and kicked her legs. He put his hand against her cheek and felt her relax. She nuzzled against him.

"Don't leave me," she whispered.

He watched her face to see if she was awake. Her chest rose in even breaths.

Jaxx didn't know what to make of the reaction, but he felt a connection to her. For so long, he'd felt the chaos around him. It had gotten to the point it was all he felt. The Federation, with their hold over Shelter City, seemed to be locked in an eternal struggle with the shifters. He desperately wanted it to end, but not in the way Fiora predicted. Not with the death of all those in Shelter City.

And, still, maybe that was the only way to end the stalemate and get the Federation off his planet. He could see no other way, and he had looked. The Federation was too powerful.

But there were so many Cysgodians in the city, so many lives, so many who did not deserve such a harsh fate.

Letting them die was not an option.

Letting Fiora go back to the general was not an option.

Doing nothing was not an option.

There were no options.

What path could be chosen when there was no path?

Jaxx looked up at the ceiling. For a dragon, when there wasn't a path that meant flying up. If the Federation smuggled people onto the planet, perhaps he could smuggle them off? How long before people noticed the missing population? How many could they free?

He'd discussed the idea at length with his parents and the Var princess, Payton, but every time they'd shot it down. A spaceship big enough to fit everyone wouldn't be stealthy, even if they could convince a distrusting population to board. Not to mention they'd break the agreement by helping them escape.

There was no winning, only varying degrees of losing.

"Fiora?"

Jaxx picked up the softly spoken word before the door to the guest suite opened. Salena appeared, glancing around the spacious room before her eyes finally found him.

"Jaxx? What are...?" Her gaze went to her sleeping sister. "What's...?"

Jaxx refused to stand. He moved his touch from Fiora's cheek to hold her hand. "She asked me to stay."

"What?" Salena crept closer, not hearing him.

Jaxx didn't want to wake Fiora. "She asked me to stay with her."

"She did?" Even with her surprised statement, Salena had to believe him. No one could lie to her. "That's unusual. Why you? Why didn't she send for me?"

"I calm the visions," Jaxx answered. He lifted his hand. Fiora mumbled in her sleep. He returned his touch, and she settled.

"That's... I don't know what that is." Salena kept her voice quiet as she sat across from him on the circular couch and leaned forward. "I came to tell her what happened. The queen was incredible. I think Fiora will find the way the general stomped off amusing. He looked like a pouting child. I thought it would lift her spirits."

"She already knew. She said she saw it in the timelines," Jaxx answered. Half his attention was focused on where Fiora's skin pressed to his. "She wants me to take her back to the general."

"What—*why*?" Salena stiffened. "She can't go back there. That makes no sense unless it has something to do with those doomsday visions she's been mumbling about. I wanted to let her rest before asking her about them."

Jaxx nodded. "Yes. She thinks it might save Shelter City from destruction if she is returned. The general won't take losing today lightly."

"No, I don't suppose he will," Salena agreed. She took a deep breath and held it for a long moment before letting it go. "We can't give her to the general."

"I have no intention of letting her go back." Jaxx tried to hide any hint of possessiveness in his tone, but Salena pulled it from him with her very presence.

Salena smiled knowingly. "You're attracted to my sister."

Jaxx tried not to answer but found the word forced from his throat. "Yes."

"I suppose it makes sense." She crossed her arms over her chest and leaned back. "I mean, you couldn't have me, so you go for her."

"That's not—wait, what?" Jaxx frowned.

Fiora stirred and he glanced down to find her staring up at him. She slowly sat up. "You are in love with my sister?"

"He asked me to marry him," Salena said. "I said no."

"It wasn't like that," Jaxx answered.

"Did you ask me?" Salena demanded.

"Yes." The word pried from his throat. "But it

was a joke because my mother, and then the bridal ceremony, and we were getting ready to smuggle food simulators because the other cache was raided and..."

Fiora arched a brow at his rambling explanation. Salena started laughing.

Jaxx looked at the two sisters, feeling as if he was outmatched.

"He's right. It was a joke," Salena relented. "His mother was on his case about losing his crystal and not taking the breeding ceremonies seriously."

"You have ceremonies for breeding?" Fiora's gaze started to drift down his body, but she caught herself and corrected course to look at her sister instead.

"Breeding festival is the old term used in the hope that the marriages would be blessed with children. Until my generation, the radiation from the sun suppressed our ability to have female dragons. My ancestors made a deal with aliens to bring compatible women once a year in hopes that matches could be made."

"I'm not sure if that's sad or strange," Fiora answered, rubbing her temple. Under her breath, she said, "Sorry, I know that sounded rude. Comments just slip out."

"You never have to apologize for speaking the

truth," Jaxx assured her. He never really stopped to contemplate just how strange their traditions must seem to the outside world. Now, with the questions reflected in Fiora's expression, he couldn't think how best to explain the old ways. "The ceremony is how my parents met, how the king and queen met. That's how most of the older generation found each other. Galaxy Brides contracted women to come to the ceremony to try their fate."

He always assumed he'd meet his mate in a similar way. But the death mark hung over his head, lingering over every decision he would make from this moment forward. He could not bind himself to a woman only to leave her, no matter how much pain it caused him.

"They officially changed it to a mating festival," Jaxx said, hoping to end this course of conversation soon. "Though I supposed that might not sound much better."

"Blue radiation from one of the planet's three suns," Fiora said, closing her eyes. She no longer touched him and gave a slight moan as she pressed her fingers to her temple.

"What do you see?" Salena asked.

"Reels of people's lives, moving and weaving into each other. There are several threads in

Shelter City pulsing with fear of blue radiation. People are worried about it, but then someone named Nadja proves that it's not harmful in the way they suspect. The Federation releases information about Nadja's father, who was a leader in the medical mafia, to discredit her. Her research is disregarded in public opinion though it was most likely correct."

"You're sure?" Jaxx asked.

Fiora opened her eyes. "I think so. I feel as if I was drifting in a dreamless sleep. It helped. Everything seems a little more organized now, not all twisted and knotted in my brain. Does that name Nadja mean something to you?"

"Princess Nadja is my aunt. She's a scientist. She came up with an immunization for the yellow, a plant that grows in the forest and causes people to pass out if they breathe in the spores. It wouldn't surprise me if she discovered the blue radiation doesn't harm the Cysgodian people like the Federation wants them to believe."

"Harm?" Fiora shook her head. "No. This doesn't make sense. Maybe the timelines are still jumbled and too hard for me to decipher. Didn't the blue sun cure them?"

"When they first arrived. It saved them. Now the

Federation insists the cure is also shortening their lives," Jaxx answered.

"Fiora, what do you see for the people of Shelter City?" Salena asked.

"I..." Fiora trembled as if she didn't want to answer but was compelled by both her curse and her sister's gift. "It's all broken, gaps in the current. Some are scared and don't want to cause trouble for fear it will be worse. Others want to riot and take down the Federation base. A sect believes shifters are the enemy, and they wish to consume them." Fiora gagged and clutched her stomach. "Their leader thinks shifter blood will give them strength and long life. They're furious and immune to reasoning."

Jaxx stared at Fiora's face, not liking what Salena's question was doing to her. He started to reach for her, but Fiora lifted her hand to stop him.

"It's all right. I want to help," Fiora said.

"Is the leader named Doyen?" Salena asked. To Jaxx, she said, "Yevgen warned Payton and me about him when we were in the city."

"Blood. Blood. Blood," Fiora whispered as if trying to grab onto a thought. "I hear the chanting." She gagged. "I get the impression that they are going to succeed soon."

"Is that what causes the explosion?" Jaxx asked.

"I can't see it," Fiora said. "I need to be closer to the city to get the rest of the readings and fill in the gaps."

"You can't go back there," Salena denied. "What else do you see?"

"Federation soldiers are angry. Something has been taken, and they have to find it," Fiora whispered.

"Do you mean you?" Salena asked.

"I don't know. They're searching. There's a woman. They'll hit her." A trickle of blood came from Fiora's nose. "She's so hungry. They all are. Hungry for food, for freedom, for..."

Fiora gasped. A second trickle came from the other nostril to drip down her chin.

"That's enough," Jaxx decided. He wrapped his arms around Fiora and pulled her to him. He made sure to touch her skin. Her face pressed against his chest, and he felt his grip tightening as if his hands were unwilling to let her go. His heartbeat quickened, and he had to focus on keeping his breathing steady. Something about this woman made the dragon simmer to the surface. He had to fight the urge to shift and fly her away to the northern mountains where he could keep her safe.

Fiora made a weak noise against him before

sighing with relief. Her body relaxed as the visions released her. Fiora's words were muffled as her face pressed against his chest. "I'm sorry, it's—"

"You don't have to apologize," Jaxx interrupted, holding her tighter. "You did what you could."

"He's right. You need to take it in smaller steps," Salena agreed. "You've said enough."

He considered the impulse to carry her away for a moment. He had cousins who lived in the mountains. Mirek and his wife had been taking care of orphans since Riona lost their baby. Sure, Fiora wasn't a child, but they wouldn't turn her away if he asked. They'd keep her safe and far away from the general.

Fiora pushed against his chest, and he was reluctant to release his hold on her. "No. I haven't. I—*oh, blast it all.*"

Jaxx let her pull away but kept his hand on her to stop her visions. If he were honest with himself, he kept touching her because he didn't want to let go. The press of her against his chest remained like a ghost against his flesh.

"I can't go back to the general," Fiora stated.

"I agree. You—" Jaxx began.

"That's not even an—" Salena tried to say at the same time.

"No, you don't understand. It's not about me. I have the Cysgodians in my head. If he asks me, I'll tell him everything. They'll inject me with boosters and pull people in front of me one by one until I know everything. I'm surprised they hadn't started trying that already. I think the general's ego prevented him from thinking the Cysgodians were a threat." A tear slipped down her cheek. "I don't see how to help them. If the Draig don't give me back, the general will be angry and will take it out on the city. But if I go—"

"You'll tell them all of the Cysgodians' fears and plans," Salena concluded for her.

Fiora nodded. "I'm too dangerous now. He'll make me tell him everything."

Salena sat back in her seat and rested her head so that she stared at the ceiling. She took a deep, audible breath.

Fiora turned her attention to Jaxx. "There is only one answer."

Jaxx stiffened, not liking the look on her face.

"What's that?" Salena asked, her attention still focused upward has she kept her head back.

"I have to die," Fiora said.

Salena jerked her head forward.

"Show my body to the general," Fiora added. "Let him know it's over."

"No," Jaxx managed. It was the only sound he could push out from his squeezing lungs. It felt like she'd kicked him.

Fiora's eyes were moist, but she smiled at them. "It's all right. I'm not scared. I—"

"We're not considering it," Salena stated. "I just found you. We have to find our other sister. Piera is still out there. We have too much work to do. Your death doesn't solve anything."

At that, Fiora gave a humorless laugh. "You forget, sister. You can lie. I can't."

"But you can be mistaken," Salena challenged. "Sure, death is the great fix for everything, a jump into nothingness, but that is not how we were raised. Life is worth fighting for. If our parents—"

"Don't bring them into this," Fiora snapped, standing from the couch to tower over her sister. "They couldn't protect us, and I couldn't save them. All these threads in my head and I couldn't have a hint of one to warn me that danger was coming. I couldn't stop it—not their murder, or the fire that burned our house, or the black holes that sucked you, me, and Piera into them and cast us out into the universe as orphans. All I'm good for is reliving it, detail by detail, for the sick pleasure of General Sten, which is why I'm not scared of dying. I might not be able to see my future, but I don't have to be psychic to know what it holds. In it, I'm being forced to see things I don't want to see and tell secrets that are not mine to tell. I'm done."

Jaxx clenched his fists. "Salena is right. Death is not the answer."

Fiora glanced at him, and he could see her frustration. Blood stained her face, smeared from when she'd pressed against him. "Then what is? Because I can't see any other path."

"Then..." Jaxx tried to come up with a solution, anything to change her course of thinking. He refused to accept that what she said was true, even though only truth could pass her lips. "We don't have enough information."

"Right," Salena jumped on his words. "If you don't see another way, then that's because we need to know more about what might cause this destruction. You said it yourself. You need to read more people. We can do it on your terms, under your control, however you need to be the most comfortable."

"And we don't know if your death would end it." Jaxx clung to any argument that would change her mind. "But if we lost you, then we lose any chance we have of figuring it out."

"So, we need you," Salena said.

"Yes," Jaxx agreed. "We need you, Fiora. Don't give up hope."

"I'll go speak to Grier. We'll leave for Shelter City at once," Salena stated. She stood and patted her sister's arm as she passed by her to go to the door. "I'm not going to rest until you feel safe enough to never wish for death again."

Fiora stared after her sister and whispered, "She doesn't understand what she's asking of me. She doesn't understand how bad it's gotten when I see things. She still sees me as her sixteen-year-old sister."

"I don't see a clear solution when it comes to the people of Shelter City," Jaxx said, "but I will not force you to go. It is not your responsibility to fix what is broken there. If anyone tries to make you, I'll take you to the forest and hide you. Say the word."

Fiora smiled at him, but she seemed so sad, and the look did not reach her eyes. He wanted to erase that sadness from her. "You don't know how tempting that sounds to be away from the world, but the world always seems to find me. I can't live with myself if I don't at least try to help those people."

"Then I promise not to leave your side." If this was how he met his end, so be it. Fiora might hold the key to ending the Federation's hold on Shelter City. "For whatever reason my presence stops your visions. So I will be there to do that. And if anyone threatens you, I will be there for that. I give you my word. You will never belong to the Federation or anyone again."

"I believe that you will try," she said.

9

"I'M COMING WITH YOU."

Fiora glanced over in surprise as a woman appeared next to her on the narrow path. They were just out of view of the palace's front gate, around a bend of trees. Mischievous brown eyes met hers. The woman's brown hair wove in an intricate pattern around the top of her head like a crown. She had a wildness to her that appeared poorly contained within a beautiful prison.

Fiora and Jaxx had just left the palace. Unlike the time Jaxx led her through the hallways, he was now fully clothed in dark pants and a red tunic shirt. He'd guided her around a maze of halls so she could avoid running into people, which she thought was sweet. The clothes he had given her to wear were close in design to his, pants with a fitted shirt and boots.

"Which one are you?" the woman asked pointedly. "Future queen or sister?"

Fiora instantly became flooded with images of the woman locked in a battle with a man she couldn't see. Wings ripped from her body before she swooped from a tower and attempted to chase after a cat running away from her.

"This is Fiora." Jaxx placed a hand on her shoulder. His finger touched her neck and pulled her out of the vision. "Fiora, meet my cousin, Princess Grace."

"You're a dragon," Fiora said. "One of the rare females I've heard about."

"And you have visions," Grace answered.

"Don't," Jaxx warned.

"What?" Grace blinked, trying to look innocent and failing.

"She's not a fortune teller," Jaxx stated.

"Well, from what I heard, she kind of is," Grace quipped.

"You should go back to the palace," Jaxx said. "You cannot be involved in what we're doing."

"What are you doing?" Grace asked.

"It's better that you don't know," Jaxx answered.

"Jaxx, Grier, and Salena are escorting me to Shelter City to see if I can read the timelines and find out what is about to kill everyone," Fiora said. "We are going to stop by Jaxx's parents' house to pick up some supplies, so no one saw us leaving the palace with bags. We did not tell the king and queen that we were leaving. We're sneaking away."

Jaxx grimaced.

Grace's eyes widened. "Really?"

"Yes, really," Fiora said. "The general is not happy that I was taken from him, and his anger will need an outlet. That could mean hurting Shelter City somehow because he knows the shifters want to help them. I can't go back because when Grier and Jaxx flew me over the city, I picked up a lot of timelines—which are what I call future premonitions because of the way they flow in my brain—and now I know too much about—"

"Grace, what are you doing?" Grier came down the path to join them. "I thought you were supposed to be getting ready to meet your—"

"No." Grace held up her hand toward Grier's face as if to block him from her view. "I am weary of you all teasing me that every time I want out of the palace, it's because the Var princes are visiting.

119

Maybe I just want out of the palace. Why should the men in the family have all the fun?"

"Because you usually *are* avoiding the Var princes when you leave the palace," Grier answered under his breath.

"Don't make me light you on fire in front of your new bride," Grace said. She turned back to Fiora. "You were saying?"

Fiora instantly answered without hesitation, "Now I know too much about the people of Shelter City and their factions, beliefs, threats, that the information in the general's hands could prove very dangerous."

"You're very..." Grace studied her, "accommodating."

"You're very aggressive," Fiora countered.

"She only speaks the truth," Grier said as if Fiora's claim against Grace amused him.

"My sister can't lie. It's physically impossible," Salena explained. "Even when we were kids all it took was one question from my parents, and Fiora told them every misdeed."

"Stop asking her questions, Grace," Jaxx ordered.

"What? Are you like her protector now?" A half-smile curled on Grace's lips. "I have a feeling Fiora can speak for herself."

"Fiora is under my—" Grier began.

"Yes," Jaxx stated, cutting off his cousin. He pulled Fiora close to his side. "I am her protector."

Fiora looked up at him.

Grace's smile widened by degrees. It didn't take a psychic to see the mischief in her. But, Fiora could also sense her pain and loneliness. She wondered if anyone else saw it, or if the impression came from the visions. "Is he more than your protector?"

Fiora didn't want to answer. "Yes. I find myself attracted to him, both physically after we landed and I followed behind him in the palace, and he was completely naked, and mentally since I discovered his touch—"

"Ah! Stop." Grace pretended to gag as she cupped her ears. "I don't want to hear it."

"—for some reason has the power to stop my premonitions from flowing," Fiora finished. "I'll probably have sex with him on multiple occasions while I have the opportunity, but sadly the future isn't looking great right now."

Jaxx cleared his throat.

Grier chuckled.

Grace opened her mouth but then shut it without saying anything.

"You asked," Salena said, hooking her sister by

the arm to lead her down the path away from the palace. "How are you feeling? You look better than when we arrived."

"Better. Frightened." Fiora glanced at the trees as the forest became thick. The trees grew wide and tall, with leaves big enough to wrap around her body. If they were to cut one down, a spaceship would be able to land on that single trunk. "Happy to not be eating nutrient paste and getting daily booster shots to amplify my premonitions." She glanced at the path. The compacted red dirt contrasted the small yellow plants growing along each side. "Being near Jaxx helps. I'm not sure what it is about him that stops the visions, but it might be because he has a death mark."

Salena stopped suddenly, causing Fiora to realize what she'd said.

"Death mark?" Grace demanded. "Is that what it sounds like?"

"Jaxx?" Grier insisted.

"It's nothing," Jaxx dismissed.

"Fiora?" Grier gently took her arm so she looked at him. "What does it mean that Jaxx has a death mark?"

"I don't want to answer you," she said, only to add, "but his future is silent. I see nothing when I look forward, only darkness. That always means one thing. There is no future." She drew her eyes to Jaxx's dark ones. "I wish it were different."

What she didn't say is that she hoped in changing the fate of Shelter City, they might find a way to change his destiny as well. Though, darkness meant his death was sooner than that of the Cysgodians. They still had timelines to show her.

"Maybe you're wrong," Grace insisted, her expression begging Fiora to recant.

"This isn't about me. This is about helping Shelter City," Jaxx said. "Payton has a contact in the city. I think I know where to find her. She can take us there, and maybe then we can narrow down which timeline will be the most useful to trace."

"Yevgen?" Salena asked.

Jaxx nodded.

"Payton took me to see him. That's how we found you," Salena told Fiora. "Yevgen monitors the city and knows everything that is happening. He might be able to help you fill in the gaps. I'm pretty sure I can lead you to where he lives."

"Yes. I agree. Yevgen. That way we're not caught roaming the city aimlessly," Grier agreed. "Salena, I'd like you to stay with Grace when we go—"

"Like hell," Grace snapped. "I'm going with you.

If you try to leave me behind, I'm telling King Ualan all about this adventure."

"Yeah, that's not happening. I'm not leaving my sister's side." Salena took up Fiora's arm again.

"Discuss it later," Jaxx said. "I hear someone coming up the path. We need to stop talking until we're past the village, or someone will overhear us."

"Shifter hearing is more sensitive than—" Salena began to explain.

"I know," Fiora broke in.

Salena kept looking at her like she was delicate and needed protection. When she spoke, her tone lightened like she conversed with a scared child. Had she been like that when they were children? It felt borderline condescending.

Thankfully, Salena didn't ask what was wrong with her because Fiora would have said precisely that, and she had no wish to hurt her sister's feelings.

Jaxx and Grier stepped in front of her as a man came down the path. Jaxx placed his hand behind his back to keep ahold of her to stop any visions. From what she could see through the space between their arms, the man looked like some of the Draig men she'd seen outside the palace door. The princes nodded at him in greeting.

"Blessed day," Grier said.

"Blessed day, my princes, princess, ladies," the man answered pleasantly.

Fiora looked down at Grier's wrist. He wore a leather band with what appeared to be a pottery shard sewn onto it. Without thinking, she reached to take his hand. He turned in surprise at the contact.

Seeing her interest in the jewelry, he said, "We removed the pottery from your sister's leg. Now I carry a piece of her with me wherever I go."

"I remember," Fiora said. The blue glaze was one of her mother's specialties. She made the most beautiful designs. Fiora and her sisters helped to dig the clay for the pots. This very shard might have been unearthed with their hands. "Salena tripped and fell into a stack of pots ready for market. Broken pieces were everywhere. The loss in sales made meals interesting that winter."

"I didn't trip," Salena protested, just as she had as a child. "I was pushed."

Fiora reached to touch the pottery with her forefinger before letting him go. With the fondness of the memory also came a bittersweet ache for that same past. It was hard not to think of the general making her tell the story of her family's death over and over. "One of us always tells the truth, and one of us doesn't have to."

"One of us clearly has a selective memory," Salena quipped. For a moment, it was just like when they were children—bickering, teasing, happy.

"We should start walking before more people come," Jaxx said.

10

For as much as Fiora hated the silence of her traveling companions, she was also grateful for it. Silence meant they weren't questioning her. The unasked questions were etched upon their solemn faces, which only grew wearier the longer they walked. The dirt path joined up with a broader cobblestone walk through the trees. She caught a glimpse of the Draig village at the base of the mountain palace. It covered part of a valley.

Jaxx stayed close to her as if wanting to always be within arm's reach if she needed to touch him. The timelines trying to invade were manageable at the moment. She didn't *need* to touch him, but she wanted to.

"I'll probably have sex with him on multiple occa-

sions, but sadly the future isn't looking great right now."

Her stupid mouth had already revealed her attraction to him, and all she could hope is that he felt the same. It's not like she could see an upcoming preview of their time together in his future. Though, she was sure it would have been a great, sexy show if she could.

"What are you smiling at?" Salena asked.

"I was thinking of Jaxx naked," Fiora answered. Her cheeks and neck heated in embarrassment, and she was unable to force herself to meet Jaxx's gaze.

Grier coughed as if trying to cover his laughter.

"So, you really can't turn that truth-telling off?" Grace asked.

"No. If I fight it, I'll get a blinding headache that will last for days, my nose will start bleeding, and I'll blurt it out anyway." Fiora sighed. "Not pleasant."

"I would think there would be something medical you could do for that," Grace mused.

"That would imply something is wrong with her," Jaxx said. "She's perfect the way she is."

"I'm just saying if it's causing problems, isn't there some kind of brain surgery or something?" Grace continued.

Fiora tried to think of a clever riddle, but she had

a difficult time. Talking to them wasn't like telling fortunes in front of a crowd.

No, not them. Him. Jaxx.

"I tried to have my vocal cords disintegrated once when the Federation was putting me into a medical booth," Fiora admitted. "They caught the programming code and stopped it before the damage was done. It wasn't very smart of me. Anything I do to myself, they'll repair. The only thing they can't fix is death."

"Stop talking like that," Salena said.

"Please don't ask me any more about this." Fiora looked to Salena, silently begging her to get them to stop questioning her.

"I apologize. I don't mean any harm," Grace said.

"How would you like it if you were asked personal questions you were forced to answer?" Jaxx countered.

"I only thought we might find a way to help make it better," Grace said, sounding slightly defensive.

Salena gave a slight nod toward Fiora and winked. "You know, Grace, I'm curious about something. What is up with your betrothment? I heard you were engaged to a Var prince, but it sounds like you are avoiding him. When's the big wedding?"

Grace's eyes widened and seemed to flash with

an inner fire. "I don't recognize the betrothment because it frightens me to know my future has never been my own. I'm afraid that I'll be trapped in a love-less, humorless marriage to a stuffy cat-shifter prince who will try to snuff out everything that I am. I resent my parents for agreeing to the treaty, even if they didn't intend for it to hold. And I know, in the end, I'm going to be forced to marry a man I don't love for the good of the kingdoms. I will do every-thing I must to put off the inevitable."

Grace put her hands over her mouth as if to stem the flow of words.

"Not so fun when it's you, is it?" Jaxx said.

Grace shook her head. "My apologies, Fiora. I won't ask you any more questions."

"I didn't know you were frightened," Grier said.

"Shut your black hole," Grace grumbled, as she surged on ahead of them on the path to effectively cut off the conversation.

"She has a lot of anger and sorrow in her," Fiora whispered as images of Grace's future flowed through her mind. "If you could see her path, you wouldn't tease her about it."

Jaxx touched her arm, drawing her from any visions of the future. He glanced at his cousin and nodded that they should keep walking as he slowed his steps and kept her with him. When Grier and Salena followed Grace, Jaxx said, "I want you to know, I'm attracted to you, too."

"I know. I heard you tell my sister," Fiora answered. She hoped that meant they'd have sex soon. She could have tried to suppress the thought, but there was no use.

Jaxx grinned. "So, I wouldn't be pushing past allowable limits if I..."

He stopped walking and cupped her face in his hands. His eyes moved to her mouth, and he hesitated before lowering his lips to hers. His kiss was warm and gentle and way too brief.

"...did this?" he finished.

Fiora shook her head in denial. "No."

"And if I wanted to do it again? Would that be allowable?"

Fiora nodded, weakly whispering, "Yes."

Jaxx's mouth met hers in a deeper kiss. Her mind was devoid of premonitions, but her thoughts ran rampant as they all focused on him. She felt the breeze against her hands, heard the sound of the wind crashing the giant leaves together overhead. Dots of sunlight danced over Jaxx's head. She kept her eyes open, not wanting to miss a moment. With Jaxx, she couldn't predict what he would do next, and the not knowing both excited and frightened her. She wasn't used to being surprised.

"I can't do what I want at the moment. If I kiss you again, I think I might embarrass myself." He glanced around at the trees and then down the path where their companions had gone. "This is not the place."

At that, Fiora chuckled. "I'm kind of the queen of embarrassing myself. It's mortifying to answer every question asked of me. Yeah, I was staring at your ass. Yeah, I want to have sex with you many, many times. Yeah, I'm going to tell my sister, your cousins, and anyone else who asks me about it. You'd think I'd be used to it by now, but—"

He placed his finger against her lips, silencing her. "I don't mind if people know I'm attracted to you, and I will be envied when they find out you're attracted to me."

"That's not the only concern," she insisted. "If I know secrets, and people want to know those secrets... I can't be trusted. The more people I'm around, the more I see. I don't think you should take me around your parents. I should hide when we get close to their house."

He looked as if he wanted to disagree but didn't speak.

"I need you to promise me something. I can't ask my sister, and Grier would never do anything to go against his wife, so that leaves you as the only person I can ask." Fiora put her hand on his arm. "I will go into the city with you to read the futures. I promise I will try to find out what I can to help you and Shelter City, but the more I find out, the more dangerous I become—to the shifters and the Cysgodians."

He again glanced down the path before gesturing that she should walk with him.

Fiora pulled his arm to stop him. "Jaxx, I need you to promise me that you won't let the Federation take me."

"I have already said you are under my protection." Jaxx's tone changed as if her words insulted him.

"Even if that means you have to kill me," she finished the thought.

He looked horrified.

"You're the only one I can ask," she insisted.

"No," he said. "It will never come to that. Death is not an answer."

Fiora frowned. "You don't know my life or my pain. Sometimes there doesn't seem to be another way out."

He looked at her for a long moment, and she

could see he was trying to choose his words. Finally, he whispered, "You're not alone."

For perhaps the first time in her life, no words forced their way past her lips. She opened her mouth, as if ready for them to escape, but remained silent.

"You're not alone."

How long had it been since she'd felt like she wasn't alone? No one cared about her beyond what she could do for them. Everyone she'd met since she'd been forced from her home had tried to use her for some kind of gain—which team would win, what industry would thrive, perform parlor tricks for my dignitary friends. That feeling of aloneness could be all-consuming and hard to see past.

"Fiora," Salena called, appearing on the path ahead of them. She waved her hand for her sister to hurry.

"We should go," Fiora said.

Jaxx grabbed her arm and didn't let her leave. Firmly, he stated, "There is always another way. We will find it."

She wasn't sure exactly what he meant by that, but now wasn't the time to ask. He released her and began walking with her toward Salena.

"You're not alone."

His words stayed with her as they rejoined the others on the path.

"What were you two—?" Grace automatically stopped her teasing question with a look at Salena. She shook her head. "Never mind. Not asking questions."

It was too late though. Fiora already knew what the rest of the sentence was. "Jaxx kissed me and then refused to kill me."

Salena began to speak, but Jaxx lifted his hand toward her and shook his head. "Everything is fine. We're near my parents' home." He looked at Fiora. "And you're not hiding in the forest."

"It will be good to see your mother again, Jaxx," Salena said. "Olena was very kind to me after you found me. I think you'll like her, Fiora."

Jaxx's parents lived a short walk from the Draig village. The home was nestled into the trees, larger than those they'd passed in the village but unassuming and not what she'd expected for a royal couple after seeing the palace.

Grier suddenly stopped. "Do you hear that?"

Fiora tilted her head and listened. "No."

Jaxx lifted his hand in front of Fiora to stop her advance. His face changed by small degrees as if trying to shift into a dragon only to stop halfway. A ridge formed across his brow, pushing out from his forehead to create a protective line over his nose and eyes. His eyes flashed with yellow flames, and talons grew from the tips of his fingers.

Fiora's breath caught, but she wasn't frightened of him.

"It's too quiet," Grace said, inching along the path toward the house with her cousins. "Something's wrong."

Two glass doors to the home were opened wide, revealing the interior before they were close enough to step inside. One of the doors had been smashed.

"This isn't right." Jaxx's voice was gruff.

"Grace, guard them," Grier ordered as he ran toward the door.

Grace grabbed hold of the sisters and pulled them back toward the side of the home while still craning her neck to see inside. Her eyes flashed with gold.

Fiora caught a glimpse of the floor. Shards of broken glass and pottery littering the entryway.

"Olena? Yusef?" Grier yelled.

"Are you in here?" Jaxx called in his now gravelly tone.

"What's happening?" Salena whispered. "Who would do this?"

Fiora instantly picked up the future of a woman with red hair following a man as he carried a broken chair through the woods. The man glanced back, surrounded by stark sunlight and shadows, looking very much like an older version of Jaxx. For a second, she started to smile, thinking she might have picked up Jaxx's future. That meant he would survive, and they were on the right path.

"I don't think they're here." Jaxx appeared at the door, worried. "Someone tore up the house."

"Jaxx, blood," Grier called from inside.

"What does Olena look like?" Fiora asked her sister.

"Beautiful. Red hair. Flaming red. Um," Salena gestured at her own face as if trying to recall. "Green eyes. Kind of mischievous, knowing expressions. Quick wit."

Fiora felt her hopes crash. It wasn't Jaxx, but his father. She pointed toward the forest to a tree she recognized from her vision. "I think they're walking over there, or will be soon."

"Jaxx," Grace yelled. "Fiora thinks she knows where they're going."

Jaxx appeared at the door. His face was still shifted in his worry. "Where?"

"I can't believe you were going to throw that

chair into the fire pit to be burned," a woman scolded from the direction Fiora pointed. The older version of Jaxx appeared on the path carrying a broken piece of furniture. "I held our son in that chair, and if your son ever gets his act together, I plan on holding my many grandchildren in that—"

"Our son or my son?" the man she assumed was Yusef answered. "You can't have it both ways, firebird."

"He's yours when he's pissing me off," Olena quipped.

"Aunt Olena," Grace called. "Are you all right? What's going on?"

The woman instantly turned toward the home and smiled. "Grace? What are you doing...?" Her smile dropped as she saw everyone. "What's happening? Has the palace been ransacked as well? Are the villagers—?"

"Everyone's fine," Jaxx assured them, rushing toward his parents. The man-dragon features retracted back into his body. He reached to help his father carry the chair. "What happened to the house?"

"I think people were looking for food," his mother answered. "They raided the kitchen and took a few loaves of blue bread and dried wilddeor. We were in the village when it happened, trying to calm nerves after the general visited the palace."

"They tried forcing their way into the guest room doors with this chair," Yusef said. They set down the broken chair without carrying it back inside.

"And your father was trying to sneak it into the fire pit so he didn't have to fix it for me while I was retrieving the cleaning droid from its storage bin to sweep up glass shards," Olena added.

"I don't like this," Grier said, pulling Salena closer to him as if to protect her from the unseen. "General Sten and now intruders?"

"Well, either Nadja has started dabbling in making clones, or Salena found a sister." Olena looked at Fiora and then Salena.

"I'm not a clone," Fiora said, answering the implied question.

"I didn't really think you were, dear," Olena said. The woman's future wove through Fiora's thoughts. The impressions were sweeter than she was used to seeing—husband and wife holding hands, laughter as Olena ran through the forest, a stolen kiss in a crowded room. There was love here, as deep as Fiora had ever sensed before. But, also, beneath Olena's surface smoldered a fierce protectiveness—of family, of shifters, of the people of Shelter City.

Jaxx had been raised in this love. She felt a pang of jealousy, or maybe it was better classified as longing. Her parents had loved their three daughters just as deeply.

Yusef and Olena moved to go inside the home, stepping over the broken glass.

"Why are they living in the forest without protection?" Fiora whispered to Jaxx.

Apparently, her whisper wasn't quiet enough because all eyes turned to her.

Olena opened her mouth to speak but then quirked a brow. She stared at her from within the doorway. "You're not like your sister, are you? We're not compelled to answer you."

"No, I—" Fiora began.

"Fiora has other gifts," Salena put forth. The interruption reminded Fiora of when they were children, and Salena always tried to protect her from strangers finding out about her ability.

"In all my hundreds of years, we have rarely needed protection." Yusef motioned for them to follow him inside.

Looking past the broken shards scattered about the floor, Fiora found the home more welcoming than the palace. There was a luxury in the palace, yes, but here, in the woods, there was comfort. Logs from the giant trees of the forest lined up to create curved patterns along the wall. Black curtains half covered the dome window in the ceiling. Small wooden carvings decorated a stone fireplace.

"And not since we married and the war with the Var ended." Olena gestured toward the couch. "Check for glass before you sit."

"War?" Fiora hadn't picked up any hints of a shifter war in her visions. Usually, there were threads of animosity that came through after a region had been through a war. "How long ago was that?"

"I'm seventy-two, so roughly that long ago," Jaxx answered.

Fiora's eyes widened, and she looked him over. "You're seventy-two?" She then glanced at Yusef. "And you said you're hundreds of years old?"

Yusef nodded. He looked very much like his son except for his dark eyes. Jaxx's eyes clearly were inherited from his mother.

"Does it matter? Does that change your interpretation of the timelines?" Salena asked. "Is the—*event* —further away?"

"No." Fiora shook her head in denial. "I'm just surprised I was kissing someone that much older than me and didn't realize it."

"Kissing?" Olena excitedly jumped on the word

and rushed back toward them to stand before her son. "Have you...? Are you telling me that...?"

Jaxx put his hands on her shoulders. "Easy, Mother."

"Are you two together?" Olena demanded, turning her attention to Fiora. "Seriously together? Is that why you have brought her to meet us?"

"Awkward," Grace mumbled under her breath as she sat on the couch. She gave a small laugh. "Jaxx, tell your mother if you're getting married."

"You do not have to be married to kiss. No, we are not getting married. I'm afraid that is not in the stars. Your son—" Fiora began.

"—is preoccupied with other things," Jaxx put forth, stopping her from telling them about the death mark. She was grateful for the interruption.

"So, no?" Olena's expression fell. "If you're kissing, you like each other. Are you two making things more complicated than they need to be? Is this because you're planning on waiting a year for the next official ceremony? If so, don't worry about it. The whole ceremony is old fashioned anyway. You won't be the first to meet your mate outside of those parameters. You can stay in the marriage tent and go through the motions when the time comes. Now, tell me everything. We can talk through this."

"I don't know if it will be in a tent, but I will have sex—" Fiora began.

"I don't want to talk about any of this with you," Jaxx said with a glance around the room. "Do you want help cleaning?"

"Leave them be, my love," Yusef said, not answering his son as he went toward a kitchen. A counter and stools separated the open space. The Old Earth style was still popular on some planets. "We are not ones to lecture them about easy beginnings when it comes to relationships. Need I remind you about the night we met at the mating ceremony? I believe you tried to stab me in the neck."

"It was a tiny prick with a drugged hairpin," Olena dismissed with a wave of her hand. "And you survived."

"Whatever you say," Yusef answered. He opened a compartment in the kitchen and activated a cleaning droid to sweep up the glass. The unit made a low humming noise as it rolled over the floor.

"Would it help if you found your crystal?" Olena asked her son with a sideways glance toward Grace.

"It would help if you stopped pestering me about it," Jaxx said.

"Can you blame a mother for wanting her grown

son to know the love and happiness I have found with your father?" Olena asked.

"No, not for wanting it. Insisting your will on him is a different conversation," Fiora said. She gasped and covered her mouth while giving Jaxx an apologetic look.

Olena's eyes widened. She stared at Fiora for a moment, before suddenly laughing. "I like this one." She slapped the back of her hand against her son's chest. "I approve. She has fire."

"Thanks," Jaxx said, smiling at Fiora. "I like her, too."

"Seriously, though, there is something about you." Olena narrowed her eyes. "You're not like Salena. What are you like?"

"I get premonitions, and I can't lie," Fiora answered. "When people ask me what the future holds, I have to answer, even if I don't want to, or I know they won't want to hear it."

"Interesting," Olena said more to herself, before adding louder, "the two of you make quite the set, don't you? No wonder General Sten is hot to have you both. A natural interrogator, and a predictor who can't lie about what she knows. It's fortunate that fate has brought you to us. I can't imagine what would happen if that power was in the wrong hands."

"We'd be forced to advance the agenda of evil men," Fiora answered. Her hands shook a little, and she clasped them together.

"There is evil in the universe. I've seen it first-hand," Olena touched Fiora's cheek, "but you're safe here. It might not feel like it, but I promise you are."

"Aunt Olena was a space pirate before she landed here," Grace said with a grin. "Sailed the high skies looking for trouble."

"Speaking of sailing the high skies looking for trouble, what is this about you firebombing your cousin off the watchtower?" Olena asked.

Grace made a small noise of dismissal. "He deserved it."

"Oh, hey," Salena exclaimed, hopping out of the unit's way as the cleaning droid came close to her feet. "You said you thought they were looking for food, but do you know *who* did this? Do you think it was someone from the village?"

"I doubt this is the work of shifters unless some of the marsh farmers drank too much of their product and became lost in the forest looking for their stills," Yusef said. "Normally, you can smell them coming. Or lingering, for that matter."

"It has to be Cysgodians," Olena answered with a pointed look at her husband.

"How can you be sure shifters didn't break in?" Fiora asked. It didn't feel right to assume automatically that the Cysgodians did it without proof. "If they were hungry enough...?"

Her words trailed off.

"Why don't you all answer her questions?" Salena asked to force them to explain. "We're asking my sister to go to the city to read futures to help all of us. She should at least know what she's stepping into."

"We're sure because it is not our way to let our neighbors go hungry," Yusef said.

"We take care of our own," Grier added. "It's a matter of honor. If someone is hungry, we make sure they are fed. If their home is destroyed, we build them a new one. If a child is left without a parent, they are taken in by a family. In this way, we all thrive."

"That is why you let the aliens come here in the first place, isn't it? The Cysgodians needed help, and as a matter of honor, you helped them because it was the right thing to do." Fiora nodded in understanding. "And that is why the general was always frustrated with the limits you set for the city. He's trying to find a way to expand his territory."

"My uncle King Ualan, and King Kirill of the

Var cat-shifters, could not deny so many people in need," Jaxx said.

"Any more than they could have killed the aliens themselves," Grier added. "But I don't think they realized the invisible strings that were attached to the deal they signed."

"It is not just the fault of the kings. All of the royals from my generation agreed to it, knowing that the Federation could not be trusted. There was no other decision we could make. Letting an entire population die over our dislike of the Federation was not something any of us could live with. An alien plague besieged them," Yusef said. "The radiation from our blue sun has healing properties and aids in our long lives. It worked. It healed them. For that, we are grateful."

"We agreed to help them recover, not this," Olena said. She spoke with more force than her husband, but Fiora got the impression Yusef could hold his own despite his laid-back temperament. "The Federation was not supposed to be here for decades."

"So the Federation was not here before, at all? That's unusual," Fiora said.

"Until then, we had kept ourselves free of the Federation Alliance," Grace put forth. "Do we need to go over this history lesson? What's done is done."

"Yes, we do," Salena said. "Keep talking."

"The Federation claimed squatters' rights because they had dominion over the makeshift city," Grace said with a frown toward Salena. "We refuse to agree that city was anything more than a temporary settlement—to do so would be to accept the alliance. As long as it can be argued that the Cysgodians are not recovered, the Federation can stay. If you want my opinion, the Federation is keeping them sick. It's why they refuse to give them medical treatment and food."

"We can complain all we want about this political battle, but we all know who the real victims are. The Cysgodians should be allowed to choose their own futures, whether it be in space, Shelter City, or settled somewhere else on this planet away from Federation rule."

Fiora closed her eyes. Their futures converged on her. She saw Grace running through Shelter City in a cloak with another woman. Fire lit the sky as a dragon flew overhead. Unfortunately, these images weren't helpful.

Jaxx lightly touched her arm, stopping the visions.

She glanced up at him. "There are too many people in Shelter City. The walls cannot hold them all. I sense the restlessness."

"Yes," Grier said. "The city has grown beyond its intended size. The Federation keeps sneaking people into the city against the treaty, but we can't prove it. We've long suspected that it happens the one night of darkness a year when the Draig are distracted with their sacred ceremony."

"I don't know if it helps, but they did not bring me here when the planet was dark," Fiora said.

"The most immediate problem is that we need to get those food simulators established in the city," Olena said. "If Cysgodians are risking leaving the city and traveling this far for food, then things have gotten worse than we realized. This has to stop."

"Payton's contact might have a lead on who stole the cache," Salena said.

"We were just in Shelter City," Grier said, stepping out of the cleaning droid's way. When Yusef frowned like he would say something, he added, "I know we didn't have permission, but we had to go to rescue Fiora."

Yusef audibly sighed. He looked as if he wanted to scold them like children but held back. "Just don't tell my brothers you were actually inside the actual valley city. Hopefully, you were not seen, and no more needs to be said. It's bad enough that you were spotted breaking into the stronghold." He gave a meaningful look at Grace. "And you, especially, cannot be caught in the city. Your father—"

"I can handle myself," Grace interrupted, stiffening in her seat and coming forward.

"Oh, I know you can, fierce one. You have nothing to prove to me, but we cannot help the burdens we are born with, and yet they are ours to carry." Yusef crossed over to her and placed his hand on her cheek. "You did not ask for your destiny, and for that, I will be forever sorry. I don't expect you to take comfort in the fact you helped to save all shifters before you were even born and continue to save them now."

Grace nodded and averted her eyes. Fiora could feel the anger and frustration coming off her in waves.

"And if that wedding day ever comes, I'll do whatever I can that is in my power to stop it," Yusef stated.

"No," Grace whispered. "You won't. I won't let you. If that day comes, it means there are no other options."

"We don't need to talk about this." Jaxx took the

attention from his cousin. "Let's focus on what we need to do now."

Grace gave Jaxx a slight nod of thanks.

"If we recover the simulator cache, and add the load we just received, we should have enough units to feed everyone," Jaxx continued. "Whoever stole them hasn't turned them on, so they're not distributing food. Cyborgs scan the city and the borders. If they detect the units, they'll punish anyone hiding them and destroy the simulators. If they catch people leaving the city to retrieve food supplies, they'll kill them. It's hard finding someone willing to risk it but we do have a few brave food runners."

"Or the thief is paying off someone to overlook the fact he's turning on a food simulator," Salena said.

Fiora moved away from Jaxx. A prickling of apprehension ran up her spine as a new timeline came into focus. She heard the crunching of plants beneath her feet. "Someone will be passing by the house. Through the woods. They're lost and going back and forth, desperate not to be seen. They are carrying..." She closed her eyes tight. "No, there are two of them—a man and a woman. They're carrying something dangerous. It is making one of them nervous."

"When?" Salena asked.

Fiora tried to look at the way the sunlight fell on the ground in her vision, and then opened her eyes and hurried to the broken glass door. "Soon, maybe. Or this time of day in the future. I..." She closed her eyes again. "I'm not sure. How long will it take to repair this door?"

"It'll be done today," Yusef said.

"Then they're coming today," Fiora answered, pointing in the direction from which she knew they'd appear. "They'll be hiding in the trees."

When she turned, all of the dragon-shifters' eyes had shifted, and they stared at the door with their heads tilted, listening. Grace had risen from the couch. Grier had his arm in front of Salena to block her movements. Yusef stood beside his wife. Jaxx had moved closer to her and motioned for her to step back.

Olena whispered, "Salena, Fiora, you're with me. Upstairs."

"Go," Grier urged Salena.

Fiora glanced at Jaxx. There was so much fear inside her, and she knew that it wasn't all her own, but she couldn't pinpoint the source. He nodded that she should follow Olena. Fiora wasn't looking for his permission.

Olena rushed up the stairs to the walkway along the second level. Fiora was slower to follow as she tried to focus on the future of whoever was coming toward the house. The center of the room was open so that Fiora could see the shifters from above. She heard a gentle tap as Olena pressed a scanner, then the sliding of a door.

Fiora clung to the rail, staring at the broken door. Salena tried to pull her arm, but she jerked away and refused to move. Apprehension grew. She felt the worry of those below, but also the excitement of a fight. The primal thump of heartbeats sounded in her ears like drums.

"Fiora," Salena whispered, tugging at her arm.

"Stop touching me." Fiora shook her sister off, trying to concentrate past the emotions.

The sound of the cleaning droid rolled across the floor. Yusef's body shifted into the form of an upright man-dragon as he moved past his son, touching Jaxx on the shoulder. He looked like a cross between a full dragon and a man, as if his body stopped halfway.

Jaxx also shifted into a man-dragon rather than a flying one and followed his father from the house. Fiora leaned over the rail to try to watch him. Grace darted after them, shifting into a woman-dragon as she ran. Grier glanced up at them before joining the others.

"They're not flying?" Fiora asked.

"Only the youngest generation can fly," Olena answered. "We call what you just saw a half shift."

As the dragons moved away from where she stood, the impressions from the woods deepen. Sending them changed the future and the couple no longer made it to the house. A man held a jagged piece of glowing metal. Cloth wrapped one end to create a hilt. Suddenly the landscape blurred as the man surged forward.

She felt pressure on her hand as the blade found a target. She caught a surprised expression as the warm sensation of blood against her skin felt so real, she jerked back and flung her hands in the air to get away from it.

Fiora tripped. As the vision faded, she felt herself falling toward the stairs. Salena grabbed her arm to stop the fall.

Fiora didn't think as she tore from her sister's grasp. She ran down the stairs, knowing she'd sent one of the dragons to their death. If she'd have kept her mouth shut, they wouldn't be in harm's way now.

11

THE FEEL OF FIORA AGAINST HIS MOUTH wouldn't leave him. It stayed with Jaxx as he moved stealthily through the trees like a blessing upon his lips. He felt himself being pulled back to her if only to be in her presence.

Fiora had said danger was coming, and they'd listened. He trusted her without thought or hesitation. Though, he could hardly credit that sensation as otherworldly when everything she said was the truth.

Each step took him farther away from her, and he was glad she was in the safety of the house.

The familiar sounds of their footsteps were like signatures marking the members of his family. They kept pace through the trees. To his right, he heard his father. Grace approached on his left. Grier followed behind.

Jaxx focused his hearing, listening to the trees. He heard the brush of leaves in a rhythmic pattern as if someone moved through them. The sound underscored the louder crashing of leaves overhead.

Grace picked up her pace, breaking formation.

Before he could react, heavy thuds came from behind.

Thump. Thump. Thump.

The sound caused him to hesitate. Why was someone coming from the house? His mother wouldn't chase after them, not with two others to protect. That left Salena and Fiora.

"Don't move," Grace ordered.

His cousin's voice spurred Jaxx back into action.

"Put it down," Grace insisted. "I don't want to hurt you."

A grunting noise answered Grace.

Jaxx found his cousin standing behind a couple of trees. Her back was to him, her hands lifted at her sides. A blue glow outlined her body. She stood in her half-shifted form, the armor of her dragon flesh protecting her human shape. If she were to shift fully, she could have firebombed whoever she faced. They wouldn't have stood a chance against her.

The thudding steps sounded from behind them. His father motioned that he was going to stop the runner from passing.

"You're safe," Grace said, her words softening to indicate she was letting the dragon slip from her features to face them as a woman. He heard the quiver in her voice. Whatever she faced frightened her. "Please, don't do whatever you're thinking."

"I won't let you..." The shaky response revealed a female.

The thudding steps ended, and for a moment, Jaxx thought his father had stopped whoever had come after them.

Swish. Thump. Thump...

He'd assumed too soon. Someone dove through the brush behind him. The footfall quickened, the gait more uneven than before as the person went off the path.

Jaxx moved toward his cousin. Grace should not have dropped her shift to leave her body exposed. The dragon armor would protect her from an attack.

"Stop!" Fiora's voice shot past him.

Jaxx instantly obeyed her command even though he didn't know if it was meant for him. But he was the only one to do so. Sounds erupted all around.

Fiora dove past his line of vision, through the

underbrush toward Grace, and directly into danger. Jaxx sprung back into action. He leaped between two trees. The strange blue glow intensified.

Jaxx roared in warning. His talons stabbed into the trunk as he propelled himself toward his cousin.

A Cysgodian woman in tattered clothing lunged at Grace. The blue glow came from her roughly hewn blade. He'd never seen such a weapon.

Fiora slammed into Grace, thrusting her out of the way as a man jumped from behind a tree. He too wielded a blue blade. Because she was in her human form, his aim would have stabbed Grace in the heart. Instead, the knife found its target in Fiora. The force of the blow changed Fiora's course, and she did not follow Grace to the ground.

Grace smacked her head into the base of a tree with an ugly thump. Fiora staggered on her feet. The knife stuck in her shoulder. The smell of burnt flesh became unmistakable.

Jaxx felt the wound as if it had happened to him. The dragon raged inside him. He roared violently, the sound tearing from his throat.

The assailant hurried toward the Cysgodian woman, taking her blade and shoving her behind his back.

Jaxx instantly went toward the couple, ready to

rip the man's head from his body. Grace remained on the ground, unmoving.

"Stop." Fiora stumbled toward the man, protecting him as she put her body in front of Jaxx. It looked as if she tried to lift both arms, but blood ran down her side, and one limb merely shook. "Help them."

Help them?

Jaxx wanted to shred the man into a thousand pieces. He heard his father and cousin joining them. Grier went to Grace and pulled her unconscious body to safety. Yusef stood beside his son, ready for battle.

"Protect the babies," Fiora said, her words gasping.

She turned toward the man and reached for his blade. The man flinched and jerked his arm back. Jaxx smelled fear. It permeated the forest like a rotting corpse.

"Help them protect the babies." Fiora's voice was calm, and that calmness seemed to affect the man. He dropped the second blade and stepped back. The woman wrapped her arms around him as if desperate not to be separated. It was then Jaxx saw her pregnant belly poking through the rags she wore.

"Fiora?" Salena cried from somewhere beyond them, searching for her sister. "Fiora!"

"Help them," Fiora pleaded. She pulled the knife from her shoulder and dropped to her knees. The bleeding became more profuse.

Jaxx swept her into his arms before she fully hit the ground. Mindful of the wound, he shifted and carried her into flight. As a dragon, he held her to him, trying not to jar her as he flew as fast as he could toward his parents' home. He saw his mother on the path below and watched as she turned to run back to the house.

Panic choked him as he landed outside the broken door. He didn't stop to consider his actions as he scooped Fiora into his arms and ran up the stairs. His mother kept a handheld medical unit in the guest suite. A medical booth would have been preferred, but the handheld could stop the bleeding.

"Don't leave me, Fiora," Jaxx whispered, balancing her in his arms as he tried to input the code to open the door. His hand trembled, and it took longer than it should have.

Rushing inside the moment the door slid open, he lay Fiora on the bed and ran to get the unit from its place inside a wall cabinet. No other fear in all his life had struck him so profoundly as this moment. He smelled the copper of her blood, felt it cooling against his naked chest. Rage toward the man who'd stabbed her churned like fire inside him. It was nothing compared to the idea of losing her.

Clumsy hands somehow managed to find the unit and turn it on. He crawled partially over her on the bed and pressed it against her wound.

Her pale face appeared kissed by death. Blood loss turned her lips a horrible shade of blue. He stared at her chest, trying to gauge whether or not she breathed.

Jaxx died a thousand times in that hellish moment. Was this the mark she spoke of? Was this soulish agony the death she'd predicted? Because to lose her would be the death of his heart. He could think of no worse fate.

"Jaxx?" His mother appeared at the door.

"I can't lose her," Jaxx whispered, unable to take his eyes away from Fiora. When the unit didn't seem to fix her, he lifted it and slammed it against the flat of his hand.

"Give it to me." Olena snatched the unit from her son and hurried around the bed. She ripped Fiora's shirt to expose the injury before pressing the unit to her flesh. The edges of the wound looked burnt as if the blue blade had cauterized the flesh, yet it still bled.

"He stabbed her," Jaxx said needlessly. His mother could easily see the injury. "Some crude blade. I'd never seen one like it."

"Who?"

"Cysgodians," Jaxx said.

"I've seen stab-burns like this before," his mother said. "It's a blade meant for cutting through harder materials. I would guess they thought it would cut through shifter skin armor."

Olena's hand shook.

"They didn't hurt anyone else," Jaxx said, assuming she thought of her husband in danger. The love his parents had for each other was strong. "It was a couple in the forest. The woman is pregnant. Fiora told us not to hurt the babies, but—"

"Then you must trust her," Olena stated. "She can only speak the truth and would have her reason for saying it. Your father will take care of it."

"How can you be so trusting?" Jaxx asked. "You barely know her."

"You trust her," his mother answered. She brushed a piece of Fiora's hair away from her face. "Why?"

"I..." Jaxx stared at Fiora. "I feel it. I feel her. I trust her more than myself. All I want is to fly her away from here and hide her from the world."

"I know." Olena nodded. "I just wasn't sure you did."

She kept her attention on healing the wound. The burned flesh began to seal shut.

"That is why I know we can trust her because I trust you," Olena continued. "I see the way you change next to her. I see the way she changes when you touch her. If your father's love has taught me anything, it is trust. And believe me, it was not a lesson I learned willingly or easily. His love..." She gave a soft laugh as if at some distant memory. "His love saved me. It taught me that the universe could be exploding all around us, but it's just noise. That kind of noise is always there, waiting to challenge us and make our lives harder. Love is a constant if you let it be. It's a ribbon that connects your father's heart to mine. And, if you let it, it will be the tie that links you to Fiora."

Jaxx thought about the death mark but refused to tell his mother about it. He did not want to cause her to worry. It wasn't as if he had answers to the unknowns—*what, when, how...?*

"Fiora saved Grace's life by jumping before the

blade. Grace wasn't shifted. She was trying to talk the woman down from her attack when the man she was with jumped out from behind," Jaxx said.

"Then our family owes her a great debt," Olena said.

Jaxx watched Fiora's chest lift with breath, but her eyes remained closed. His mother pushed a button on the unit and moved it to the side of Fiora's neck to inject her with medicine before returning it to the wound. "I can't lose her."

"You won't." Olena lifted the unit. Skin had grown over Fiora's wound. "The handheld can only do so much. She'll need a little time to rest after the blood loss."

Jaxx lifted Fiora's hand into his to make sure any dreams she had were easy ones. "I'll wait with her."

"First Salena and now Fiora. At this rate, you are well on your way to saving what is left of their family," Olena said. "Do they have any idea where their third sister is?"

"No." Jaxx sat back and lifted Fiora's hand in his. "I thought we might talk to Alek and see if he can help us. I remember hearing a story about how they found Kendall's sister when she was lost in space. Maybe they can get lucky twice and find Piera."

"That sounds like a good place to start," Olena said. "I'll get in touch with him."

Alek was his father's first cousin. He and his wife, Kendall, lived in the Northern Mountains. Two of their sons, Zavir and Thorn, were adventuring off-world. They were all around the same age as Jaxx, but Jaxx had never had that same kind of wanderlust. Mirek had taken them all up into space when they were younger so they could see what the world looked like from the heavens.

He loved Qurilixen. From the stars, the planet appeared so small, like he could hold it in his hand and protect it from the rest of the universe. Sometimes he thought about that trip, seeing the red surface dotted with clouds. Everything he cared about had been right there in front of him, some so small he couldn't see them, but there. In the concept of time and space, it was but a spec of dirt on a timeline longer than anyone could imagine. Yet, it was everything to him.

He had the same feeling now, looking at Fiora's face, that feeling of love and fear, of the desire to cup her in his hands and keep her safe where he could watch over her.

"I'll bring you some clothes before going out to meet your father to see what is happening. You stay here with Fiora." Olena patted his shoulder as he passed.

Jaxx barely registered her leaving as he stared at Fiora, unable to look away. He thought of the Federation, of Shelter City, of food simulators and freedom.

"It's just noise. That kind of noise is always there, waiting to challenge us and make our lives harder. Love is a constant if you let it be...if you let it, it will be the tie that links you to Fiora."

He understood what his mother meant, but that noise was important. It mattered. What they did in this life mattered.

If he had the death mark if his timeline was shorter than he had always believed, did it change anything? Did it mean his life had any less meaning? Did it have more?

Jaxx took a deep breath, his attention moving from Fiora's face to her healed shoulder and blood-stained shirt.

Death didn't change who he was, what he believed, what he would fight for. If anything, it sped up the timeline.

Timelines.

What an interesting way to think of things, like lines drawing out of people into the future. He saw the pain they caused Fiora, but what would it be like to see them, to know what would happen, to understand the path you were on so completely.

But Fiora didn't see her path. She saw everyone else's.

Jaxx held her hand, not letting go, hoping his touch kept the timelines from disturbing her unconscious state.

He heard the door behind him. His mother set clothes on the bed.

"I feel like half of my life has been spent making sure all you flying dragons have access to clothes," Olena mused, almost to herself, as she again left.

Jaxx and the other full dragons didn't consider their nakedness, probably because they spent half their life ripping seams and transforming back to their human forms. It's not like clothes shifted with them.

Jaxx flung the shirt aside and took the pair of loose pants. He threaded his feet through while keeping his hand on hers and managed to pull them on. Then, crawling over her to the other side, he laid down next to her. The rhythmic rise and fall of her chest held his attention, and he watched over her.

"I should have protected you," he whispered. "I promised to take care of you, and I failed. I should be the one lying here. I have the death mark. Not you."

He knew she was safe here. The handheld had healed her wound. She would live. Yet the tightness in his chest did not ease. Had the man's aim shifted by even a small degree, he would have stabbed her in the heart.

"...it will be the tie that links you to Fiora."

12

Fiora fought to stay inside the haze of her thoughts. She didn't want to leave the numb cocoon surrounding her. It felt like childhood when the air was just a little bit too cold, but it didn't matter because she could burrow beneath a warm, thick blanket. In the fog between dreams and wake, nothing mattered. There was no fear, no pain, only the lingering images from dreams soon to be forgotten.

She half expected to hear her mother's voice urging her to get out of bed. Any second the smell of morning cakes would tickle her nose. Piera would complain about having the same meal every day. Their father would take one too many, and their mother would scold him for it.

The smell never came, and she realized her blanket cocoon didn't exist. The warmth came from her side. She was no longer a young girl full of dreams and imagination. Monsters were real, and nightmares were for the living.

A shiver worked along her body at the notion, causing tiny bumps to roll over her flesh like a wave. Even as she feared the sudden rush of timelines that was sure to come, she was relieved with each passing second when they didn't.

Fiora opened her eyes. She expected to find the white of her cell wall instead she met Jaxx's green eyes. He laid next to her, his head resting on the crook of his arm. His hand stirred against hers.

"How are you feeling?" His words came out in a rush as if he'd been waiting to say them.

"Doesn't hurt." She rolled her shoulder as if to prove her point. In truth she was a little lightheaded and weak. Thankfully she was resting on her back and not expected to move.

"I want to yell at you for running into danger like that, but I am too relieved that you are recovering." Jaxx's voice was soft. His hand tightened over hers. "I should have stopped you."

"From running in front of a blade?" She shook her head slightly. "You couldn't know what I was doing. My vision sent you into the woods. It would have been my fault if they killed Grace. I had to do something, and there was no time to have a conversation about it."

"You saved my cousin." Jaxx's hand left hers and moved to touch her cheek. He remained next to her on the bed.

"I know." Fiora let her heavy eyelids close briefly. Since he touched her the visions didn't come back, but she'd already seen the brother and sister's futures. When she again opened them, she said, "I saw Grace taking those people along a mountain path. She's going to help them."

"Dulla and Brogan," Jaxx said. "Sister and brother."

A tear slipped over her cheek. Jaxx brushed it away.

"What is it?" he asked. "Are you in pain?"

"I feel for that mother. Her heart is going to give out in childbirth. Brogan will want to take them, but he can't provide for two babies on an alien world. He will agree that they should be raised by a kind couple who has been married for many years and has taken in multiple children in need."

"Mirek and Riona," Jaxx said. "They lost a child,

and she cannot have them. Mirek is my father's cousin and lives in the Northern Mountains."

"Grace will carry the guilt of not being able to save her, but there is nothing that can be done," Fiora said.

"But, if Grace knows, then we'll send the medic unit with her," Jaxx said. "You saved Grace and changed a timeline. Surely, if Grace is prepared, we can save this woman. Or we don't send her at all."

Fiora pulled his hand from her face and released him so they weren't making contact. She closed her eyes, concentrating on Grace's thread. She felt his resolve to keep the woman in his parents' house, which changed the future. "If you don't send her, the Federation will find her here. Dulla and her brother will die, the children will be raised in an orphan program run by the Federation to train soldiers. The Federation will use this as a reason to occupy the planet permanently and, in time, will spread the city's borders. It will be the beginning of the end."

As she said the words, she felt his resolve change, to send them to the mountains. That second of indecision changed the future, erasing the orphanage for the mountain paths. He evidently wanted to send the medic with Grace because the future was different than the first time.

"If you send the handheld medical unit with Grace, Dulla will have the children on a forest path. One of the children will be stillborn." Fiora saw the path, but it wasn't the same as last time. She'd disrupted the future by telling Jaxx about it. They were small changes, but those tiny ripples grew. "Grace will try to save her but will have to choose between a baby and the mother with the medical unit. The mother will have made her promise to take care of the remaining baby."

"But before, when they didn't have a handheld medic, you said both babies went to my cousin and only the mother died. How is it two may die now that Grace has the device with her?"

Fiora peeked at his concerned gaze before again closing her eyes. "Knowing of the danger changes how they react. Grace takes the trip slower, focused on the mother and watching for labor to begin. This delay causes them to become caught off guard when a hairy beast crosses their path. Dulla slips, and a child is injured in the fall."

"We'll tell Grace to fly her to the mountains," Jaxx countered.

Again the future shifted with his new plan. "Grace tries to make the trip faster, flying the mother ahead. The fear she feels being suspended above air causes labor to start. There's a bad landing."

"Then there is no hope." Jaxx let loose a long sigh. "I'm sorry. I shouldn't have asked you so many questions. I know it's painful for you."

"No, keep going," Fiora urged. The timelines hadn't hurt as badly as before, and she was able to focus on it. The strange thing was how fast the ripples between the ideas appeared. There was a calming effect to his presence. "What is your next plan for them?"

"Uh..." He hesitated. "I suppose I'd give Grace the medic just in case but not tell her what it is for."

Fiora closed her eyes. She pressed her fingers to the bridge of her nose. "Grace can't save her."

"What if I sent my father instead? Or my mother?" Jaxx asked.

Fiora shook her head. "Same result with a small variance on the path they travel."

"Grier?"

The change offered no solution. Fiora shook her head in denial.

"What if we take her?"

Again she shook her head. "No. I'm sorry."

"We'll take Dulla to the dragon palace," Jaxx

suggested. "They have a medical booth. She can give birth in the unit."

"Same results as if you left her here. Servants will whisper, and the word will eventually get back to the Federation. The children are not sent to the orphanage because they'll be under dragon protection, but Brogan will surrender in a foolish attempt to stop a war that cannot be stopped. Dulla dies in childbirth even though they have a medical booth for her."

Fiora dropped her hand from the bridge of her nose and swiped at her moist eyes to stop the drop of tears before opening them.

"It seems that no matter what we do, it's her time." Fiora stared at his naked chest. Even as she said the words, understanding them to be accurate, she hated the helplessness of knowing. "Death can sometimes be delayed, but it eventually comes. I see no delaying the mother's fate. Her past has already cast her toward this future."

"Then what can we do?" Jaxx asked.

"Nothing. The best path for the most people is to let Grace escort them to the mountains. Let brother and sister have that time together without grief. Give them that small hope of freedom." Fiora reached to take his hand, stopping all visions. Sometimes doing nothing was the most challenging task of all. "And make sure they don't speak to me before they go or I'll ruin it for them by telling them the truth."

Jaxx nodded. "It will be as you recommend."

Fiora became aware of the feel of his skin, not because it took away her visions, but the texture and heat of it. Warmth radiated from his body. No, not just warmth, an electricity she could feel snapping against her length. It called her to come closer. She might not be able to see her own future, but she knew what she wanted.

"Ask me what I'm thinking," she whispered.

"What are you thinking?"

"I want you to kiss me," she answered. "I want you to move closer."

Jaxx leaned his mouth nearer, letting the brush of his lips tease hers as he said, "Ask me what I'm thinking."

"What are you thinking?" she asked, her body tensing with anticipation.

"That I want to kiss you and move closer."

He closed the distance between their mouths. She felt protected in his embrace. His hand moved behind her back, inching her toward him so their bodies pressed together. The rise of his chest as he breathed moved hard muscles against her sensitive breasts. She became aware of his heart beating beneath her palm.

Jaxx's kiss held only pleasure. His touch kept the world from plaguing her mind. Fiora still felt a little weak from her injury, but she didn't want to stop. She wanted to live in this moment forever.

His kiss deepened, his tongue parting her lips. When he caressed her, he acted as if she might crumble. His touch remained light, his fingers kneading her clothes.

There were so many truths she wanted to speak, but only one seemed important enough to escape her lips. "I feel connected to you, Jaxx. Every second of my life has been bringing me to this moment, to you. I have seen enough of life to know that I love you."

Her words caused him to lean back so he could study her face. "I know I should not tell you I love you. It feels selfish to say knowing I will not be here..." He hesitated. "I will not be here to..."

"I may have been wrong about the death mark," Fiora said. "I can't see my future, or rarely anything that has to do with my future, so maybe that means I'm in your future."

The words came from her lips so it had to be true. There had to be a chance. Though the fact she saw nothing of his future didn't exactly support the idea. Not everything about this man's future would involve her. She should have seen something, even if it was just a small glimpse of something random.

Jaxx grinned. "I like that prediction."

"It wasn't a prediction. It was a guess," she corrected. "Or more like a wish."

"I'm going to choose to believe that's our fate," Jaxx answered, stopping any further comments with his kiss. His hands roamed over her hip and waist.

She wrapped her arm around him as they laid on their sides, feeling along his spine. The smooth skin gave no hint of the dragon beneath. She found herself concentrating on his muscles, pressing them to see if she could detect anything hidden within.

Jaxx pulled away and glanced over his shoulder. "What are you looking for?"

"Scales," Fiora answered. "Or wing bumps."

"Wing bumps?" He gave a small laugh.

"They have to retract somewhere," Fiora said, drawing her hand to his neck to cup his face.

Jaxx's eyes flashed with gold, and the sight of it gave her a small thrill. His hand roamed down her stomach before diving beneath her waistband. "While you're doing that, I'm going to look for..."

Fiora laughed, cutting off his words, but her laughter didn't last long as desire took over. His fingers found their target as they slipped between her thighs. A jolt of awareness shot over her at the intimate touch. She inhaled deeply, moving against him.

There were no timelines to interrupt her thoughts, and she focused entirely on Jaxx. Each feeling became magnified. He pushed his knee between hers, opening her thighs for better access.

Jaxx adjusted his hips, rolling her onto her back. The motion pulled his hand away, and she instantly reached to push her pants from her waist. She didn't want the pleasure to stop. He followed her lead, freeing himself from his clothes. Fiora pulled her shirt from over her head.

Jaxx settled between her now-naked legs. Fiora ran her hands over him, trying to touch everywhere at once. Everything about him mesmerized her—his smell, his touch, the taste of his warm and gentle kisses. It was as if he poured himself into her, giving her everything.

She felt connected to him like she'd never felt connected to anything. With him there were no thoughts of the future—a rare blessing. There was only the now, and now she wanted his touch to last forever.

Excitement flooded her. Her breathing deepened. Jaxx kissed his way to her ear and then moved down her neck. Calloused hands cupped her breasts, and he squeezed gently.

Fiora rubbed her legs against him, feeling the texture of his skin along the full length of her body. His kisses replaced his hands on her chest, and she wove her fingers into his hair to keep him close. Heat infused his kisses, and his golden eyes glanced up at her. The dragon simmered below his surface. Each second grew her passion.

Present. She was present.

Fiora alternated between pressing his mouth to her nipple and reaching to scratch her nails against his back and shoulders. He moved his mouth lower, working his way down her stomach to her thighs. Jaxx moaned as his hot kisses resumed on her sex, teasing her with his tongue. She pulled at his arms, trying to get him to come over her so that they may join. Her foot ran along his hip to hook around his ass to draw him closer.

Only when her body began to tremble with the threat of release did he return his mouth to hers. His thick cock bumped her inner thigh, urging her to part her legs. She eagerly thrust her hips forward.

Jaxx entered her slowly as if savoring the moment. Nothing beyond them mattered. There was no past, no future, no threats, just the glorious now.

Fiora clung to him, desperate for the release he offered. Her body teetered on the brink of climax. Jaxx thrust fully into her. She wiggled beneath him, urging him to move.

They set a natural rhythm as they joined, one that built in tempo until it became almost frantic. Fiora needed him, all of him. He pushed up on the bed for leverage. She grabbed his hips and tried to force him deeper with each pass. He didn't stop pumping his hips until they finally found that perfect moment of release.

Fiora couldn't hold back as she cried out softly. Jaxx's moan joined hers. He delved forward one last time, embedding himself deep.

Fiora could not imagine a more perfect moment. Being with Jaxx, feeling him, shifted something deep inside her. He made her feel safe. He freed her from the pain of her visions.

She wrapped her arms around him and held him on top of her. The weight of him pressed her into the mattress, making it hard to breathe. She didn't care. She didn't want to let go of him. She felt him sigh next to her neck.

"I feel connected to you, Jaxx," she whispered. "I can't explain why, but I know I'm meant to be with you."

He lifted from her and shifted his weight to the side. She deeply inhaled as he settled next to her. "My ancestors would say it's because our being together is the will of the gods."

"Fate." Fiora nodded thoughtfully. "I like the idea of having a fate."

"As do I," he agreed. "I don't need a glowing crystal to tell me what I feel. I love you, Fiora. I have since the first time we met."

"The first time we met, I..." She glanced down toward his hips and scrunched up her nose. "I'm still sorry about that."

"Think nothing of it. I would fly through the fires of Bravon for you. All I care about is that you're here and you're with me." He kissed the tip of her nose.

"I love you, too, Jaxx," Fiora said, closing her eyes and holding him tight. "I don't want to lose you. I might have been wrong about the death mark, and I pray that I am, but I know I'm not wrong about the death coming to Shelter City. The images are still there in my mind from when Grier flew me over. We need to help those people."

"Then we will help them."

Fiora hoped it was as simple as him willing it to be so. "My entire life I didn't want to see the future, and now all I wish is that I could peek into ours to know everything is going to work out. I've never been this frightened."

Jaxx held her close, stroking her naked back.

"Actually, I've never been this present in a moment," she said. "Everything is so quiet when I'm with you, and it's giving me time to think, which really means I have time to worry."

Jaxx touched the bottom of her chin and angled her mouth toward his. "I have to believe that the gods wouldn't let us find each other if we weren't supposed to be together."

13

"I was worried about you." Salena sat next to Fiora on the couch.

Olena helped Jaxx pack a bag for their trip. The low sound of their conversation drifted from the kitchen.

"I came up to check on you, but," Salena made a small noise that sounded almost like a laugh and leaned in to whisper, "when I came by the door it sounded like you were a little occupied so I didn't knock."

Fiora's eyes rounded as she got her sister's meaning. Thankfully, there wasn't a question in that statement, and she didn't give a full accounting of what had transpired in the bedroom.

Fiora still felt weak, but Jaxx watching over her

had helped her sleep. When she'd woken up next to him, he'd been holding her hand. Without a word, he'd leaned over to kiss her and make love to her again. The feel of his mouth lingered, even now.

"You were right about those people needing help," Salena continued. "I questioned them. They didn't admit to wanting to harm us. They were frightened. Grace and Yusef are escorting them to the mountains to a safehold."

Fiora touched her shoulder, feeling for a wound she knew wouldn't be there. Without Jaxx touching her, she was able to recall in full detail the pain the brother would be feeling when his sister died. "Dulla and Brogan."

"Yes." Salena nodded. "Dulla's husband was harming her. Brogan helped her escape from Shelter City. She'd tried running away before, but the husband found her."

"I don't expect anyone could hide for very long in a closed city," Fiora answered.

"I would say that's a safe assumption," Salena said. "That city is no place to raise a child. It's barely inhabitable for adults. They'll be taken care of by Grier's family."

Fiora didn't meet her sister's eyes. She wasn't

even able to nod in fake agreement. To do so would be a lie.

"You don't think so?" Salena asked, touching her arm to get her to look at her.

"No. The mother won't be taken care of. She is going to die in labor, and there is nothing we can do to stop it. Jaxx and I tried to come up with a different scenario, but sometimes things are what they are. It's the mother's time. As much as I want to, I can't stop it."

Fiora hated the feeling of helplessness that came from visions like these. She saw the woman's future change so many times, but none of the variations mattered.

"We should warn Yusef," Salena said. "If he knows, he can—"

"No. It will make things worse." Fiora wished her sister would stop, but Salena kept making suggestions, and Fiora kept seeing new versions of the mother's death.

"Yes, I promise to be careful," Jaxx said to his mother as he approached them, interrupting the conversation. "Yes, we will come back as soon as we're done."

"There has to be something we can do. We just

need to find the right combination of events," Salena insisted.

"It's not like I wish her dead," Fiora answered, standing. The tension headache had begun to build.

"I never thought you did," Salena answered.

Grier came inside in the process of pulling on a shirt. "The path looks clear for travel." He glanced between his wife and Fiora. He appeared concerned but didn't ask about it. "Should we leave?"

"Yes." Fiora went toward Jaxx and took his hand to stop the replay of the mother's death as it settled back into the original version. She took a deep breath and let it out slowly as the headache eased.

Jaxx cupped her face, clearly not caring who saw his affection for her. "You can stop at any time. Just say the word. I won't leave your side."

Fiora nodded. "Thank you. I want to get it over with. Can we go?"

No part of walking into a packed city sounded like fun, but she hoped with Jaxx by her side this time would be different. Still, there would come a moment when she couldn't hold onto him, that she would have to see the futures. And, worst of all, there was always the possibility that the death of the city would be like the mother's—inevitable, fated, horrible to behold.

But what else could she do? Didn't she have to try?

"Travel safe." Olena followed them outside.

Fiora could see the woman's concern for her family. She dropped Jaxx's hand. A vision of Olena with her husband flowed into her. "Yusef will come back to you. I see a long future."

It was the only words of comfort Fiora could offer. She couldn't see Jaxx's fate.

Olena opened her mouth, clearly ready to ask questions. Jaxx grabbed hold of Fiora's hand to stop any visions. Olena changed her mind and simply said, "Thank you."

The temperate breeze coming through the trees seemed at odds with the gravity of their task. They followed the path cut into the ground from years of foot travel. The packed red earth was dotted on each side with yellow ferns and sprouts of struggling green. Between the thick tree trunks she glimpsed fallen logs in the forest, covered with vines and moss. Fresh air mingled with the smell of decaying wood.

The thump of their footsteps didn't appear to scare off the undulating hum of insects. The noise rolled through the trees as if their song traveled like a wave over the distance before suddenly stopping. The pause lasted a moment before replaying.

Dots of sunlight came through the canopy of trees, each leaf nearly as large as her torso.

"Beautiful night for travel," Grier said.

"How can you tell it's night?" Fiora looked up at the hints of sky she could see through the leaves.

"You can tell by the color of the light, the smells, the temperature," Grier said. "It's subtle but I've been told it doesn't take long for newcomers to start to sense the changes."

"I never realized how much I'd miss darkness," Salena said.

"Mother always said monsters couldn't find us in the dark," Fiora answered. Even though the idea still made her feel safe, she knew her mother had been wrong. Monsters could find them anywhere.

"Perhaps we could install a virtual reality booth," Grier said to Jaxx.

"Yes. I'm sure there are many programs filled with nightfall. Princess Samantha still has contact with her old crew." Jaxx's hand tightened on her slightly. He adjusted the pack he carried on his shoulder, resetting the weight.

"That wasn't a hint," Salena said. "I don't expect you to build a virtual reality booth for me."

"If it would make you happy, I'd build an entire planet for you, my love," Grier said.

"Who is Princess Samantha?" Fiora asked.

"Payton's mother," Salena said. "Payton is a friend of ours, a cat-shifter. Her mother is a human married to the Var commander. Payton told me her parents met when her mother kidnaped her father and took him to space. It sounds ridiculous, but since she can't lie to me it has to be true, or at least she believes it to be."

"I don't think she's human," Jaxx corrected, "but she is humanoid."

"She was a space pirate," Grier added. "And as far as I know, the story is very true. She captained a spaceship."

"Was she on the same crew as Olena?" Salena asked Jaxx.

"No," Jaxx said. "My mother ran with a rougher crowd. From all I've heard, Samantha's crew were more gentleman pirates. They mostly did things to annoy the Federation."

Fiora didn't ask but could well deduce that Olena had run with criminals in her youth. Had they not told her, she would never have guessed.

Fiora stayed quiet as the others talked about people she had not met. Salena told her of her time on the planet, of her adventures in Shelter City, of being at the Var palace. Grier spoke of treaties with the cat-shifters, of old wars and new fears. Jaxx focused more on making sure she knew what to expect when they arrived at the city.

Jaxx held her hand so long that their palms began to feel clammy. The forest backdrop became constant in its sameness and if not for the path, she would never have known where they had come from. The path forked in three directions, and they took the left. They'd been walking for what felt like hours.

"Are we close?" Fiora asked.

Jaxx and Grier looked at her in surprise.

"We'll have to sleep in the forest," Jaxx said. "We should arrive tomorrow."

"I would have sworn it was much closer," Fiora said. "I must have been out of it when we flew to the place from the stronghold."

"Flying is much faster than walking," Grier said.

"Then why aren't we flying?" Fiora asked. She wanted this trip to be over. "Unless it's bad etiquette to assume you'd carry us?"

"Not at all. We'll gladly carry you," Grier said.

"After last time we didn't think you'd want to fly," Jaxx said.

"Because I got sick on you?" Fiora couldn't blame him.

"No, because you had visions when I touched

you in dragon form. Whatever stops them from happening didn't work when I was shifted." Jaxx lifted their joined hands and kissed her knuckles. "We can walk."

"If that is your only reservation, we should fly," Fiora said. "Selfishly, I don't want to rush because I would rather this walk last forever. I don't want to go into the city to read timelines. However, logically, I know the sooner we get to Shelter City, the sooner we will find whatever answers there are to find. Catastrophic disaster is coming, but I don't know if it's tomorrow, in a year, in three years. Though with how strong the visions were, I'm guessing it's sooner rather than later."

"I don't want to make this trip any harder on you than it has to be," Jaxx said.

"And I thank you for that, so make sure you don't toss me around too much as you fly." She gave a smile, hoping to illicit one from him in return.

"Fiora's right," Salena agreed. "We'll arrive much faster if you take us."

"Jaxx?" Grier asked, leaving it up to his cousin.

"Are you sure, Fiora?" Jaxx asked.

She nodded.

"You can change your mind at any moment," he

said. "Just tap me, nudge me, kick me, whatever you want, and I'll bring you right back down."

"I will." She nodded again.

He still looked hesitant.

"I'll be all right," she assured him.

"I won't drop you, but *if* you were to fall, put your arms out to your side, and I will grab hold of them and catch you," he said.

Fiora placed her hand on his chest. "I trust you, Jaxx."

He frowned. "And if the visions get too bad—"

"I'll nudge you," she assured him, "and you will bring me down."

Jaxx nodded.

Grier pulled his shirt over his head and handed it to his wife. He watched Jaxx as if trying to decide if his cousin would change his mind.

"I'll carry the pack," Salena said, reaching for the bag Jaxx held slung over his shoulder.

Jaxx hesitated before releasing Fiora's hand to give the bag to Salena.

"Bring me his clothes when he's done," Salena said, as she shoved Grier's shirt into the bag. She walked with Grier up the path until they were hidden from view.

"I supposed we could look at the positives of this experience," Fiora said.

"Positives?"

"You have to remove your clothes to shift into a full dragon," she said.

Jaxx glanced after his cousin and, not seeing him, stepped closer to Fiora. He cupped her face and turned her mouth to meet his. Passion poured from his kiss, but more than that, she felt his love.

"I want nothing more than to protect you," he whispered against her mouth. "I don't want to bring you into danger. I don't trust myself once I'm shifted not to fly you to a cave and hide you away."

"I know you won't do that," she said.

"The animal inside me wars with the man. I get the logic of what we're doing, but the dragon..." He pressed his forehead to hers, staying close to her. "The dragon is controlled by his primal instincts."

"To the man, I will say we must do what we have to in this life, not what we want to. I have seen the honor in you, and in your people. Neither of us can stand aside when so many lives are on the line. It is that trait I see in you, and it is your honor that makes me love you even more." She tilted her head back to give him a quick kiss before letting her forehead drop forward to touch his once more. His eyes were closed, and his breath fanned against her cheek. "To the dragon, I will say I love you, and it is because you love me that I know you will do what I need you to do. Flying me to a cave might protect my body, but it will kill our souls. We cannot find happiness at the expense of so many others. So, dragon, if you want to save me, then you have to help me."

He slowly nodded and opened his eyes. "You're right. Of course you're right."

"I know." Fiora took little pleasure in being right about this. "Now, hand me your clothes."

Jaxx gave a small laugh and did as she said. He stood straight and pulled his shirt over his head.

Her eyes went to his tattoos. "Where did you get these?"

"Some of my mother's old crew acquires certain items for us," he said.

"Like the food simulators?"

"Yes. They also brought something called Old Earth moonshine. We drank until we couldn't see our hands before our faces and then..." He lifted his arm to show his marking.

"You got drunk and woke up with a tattoo," she concluded.

"I got drunk, lost a bet, and then had to be the first to test the tattoo laser," he corrected.

"What was the bet?"

"I honestly can't remember. Moonshine has a way of blurring reality." He reached to pull out of his boots. "Though I think it had something to do with jumping into a ship's cooling tank naked."

She flinched at the very thought of it. "That's insanity. I'm pretty sure old factions used to do that to torture people."

"I thought my dragon skin would protect me." He hooked his fingers into his waistband and stopped. "Before I turn, do you want me to carry you by the arms like last time, or do you wish to ride on my back?"

"Back," she said, not wanting to dangle in the air again. "That sounds...more solid."

"I won't be able to speak to you, but I will understand you," he said.

"All right."

"I won't hurt you."

"I didn't think you would."

"I don't want you to be frightened. I'm told it can be scary to see the shift."

"Jaxx?"

"What is it?" He looked as if he might change his mind about taking her up if she but said the word.

"Take your pants off and give them to me." She gave a meaningful glance at his waist. "Stop stalling."

"As my lady wishes." He gave a small bow before tugging his pants off his hips.

Her eyes followed the gesture, and she smiled at the sexy view. "I don't think we have time to take care of your arousal, do we?"

"I hear Grier and Salena just around the corner." Jaxx looked down to where his shaft had lifted as proof of his desire for her.

"Because if we did, I am more than willing," she assured him.

"As am I, but..." He again glanced down the path.

"Fiora? Are you ready?" Salena called.

"Technically yes, but I would rather take time to have sex with Jaxx first," Fiora answered. Her cheeks heated, and she knew they were turning red at the admission. Under her breath, she muttered, "Damn my curse."

"I know the feeling, but it will have to wait," Salena said. "Tell him to shift. I'm coming in one minute to grab his clothes."

Hard, dark armor grew over his skin. It hid his erection beneath a protective layer. As fascinating as it was to watch, she was sad to see it go.

A loud pop sounded, drawing her eyes back up to

his face. Jaxx's jaw disjointed and pushed forward. Protrusions grew like spikes from his head. She flinched, imagining the pain that he must have felt. His eyes changed shape and filled with the golden glow of his shifted form. His teeth sharpened and lengthened. Talons replaced his nails, and he fell forward to the ground. Wings sprouted from his back.

"Dragon," she whispered, half in panic, half in awe. She tried to calm the beating of her heart, knowing he wouldn't hurt her, but still seeing the large beast growing before her caused her stomach to tense with a thread of fear. A tail grew behind him. It swished in the air when he flicked it.

Heat wafted through the air as he breathed, like the blast from a furnace. When his mouth opened, she saw a hint of fire burning in the back of his throat.

Was it too late to change her mind?

The first time she'd flown, she had been overwhelmed with timelines and hadn't noticed just how monstrous the dragon actually looked, or how large.

No, not monstrous. He wasn't a monster. This was Jaxx. She knew him, trusted him.

Fiora pushed her initial apprehension aside. She had no reason to fear him. The sound of breaking bones stopped, and he stretched his wings. He turned his attention toward the trees.

As the initial shock of seeing the transformation dissipated, it was replaced by another feeling—attraction. Not so much for the dragon, but for the man inside the dragon. The power of Jaxx's shift, of what he could easily become, made her feel protected. None of the general's soldiers would be able to take on a dragon.

Jaxx's wings lifted slightly. He stared at her before slowly lowering his head, as if trying to make his posture as nonaggressive as possible. Fiora raised her hand and stepped toward him to explore the feel of his skin.

"Hide those jewels, Jaxx," Salena yelled. "I'm coming."

Fiora jerked her hand away from his neck before making full contact. Jaxx lifted his head and looked toward Salena.

"Oh, good, you're ready," Salena said.

Jaxx nodded his head once.

"I find it easiest to climb on the back and grab the base of the wings," Salena said, as she picked Jaxx's clothes off the ground and shoved them in the pack. "Then hold on tight and try not to fall off."

Fiora nodded.

Salena joined her sister in front of Jaxx. She placed a hand on her arm and took a deep breath. "He'll take care of you."

"Why do you say it like that?" Fiora asked, wondering at the strange finality in her sister's tone.

"No reason." Salena turned to go, only to stop and come back. "Actually..."

"What is it?"

"I know we're not connecting like we used to. I thought when we found each other we'd click, like two missing pieces. I thought... I don't know what I thought."

"We're not the same people," Fiora said. "We can't be the same young girls we were back then. We've been through too much. I'm not the same, and I don't want to be that girl again."

"Now I have to ask, why do *you* say it like that?" Salena crossed her arms over her chest.

"Quite frankly, you were a little bossy. You liked to tell us what to do," Fiora said. This didn't feel like the perfect time to have a heart-to-heart conversation with her sibling. "I couldn't lie to you so you always got the answers you wanted. Piera was too kind-hearted to go against you. She liked having her decisions made for her. You can lie to us, so you could convince us to do things."

"I..." Salena's mouth hung open for a few seconds before she snapped it shut.

"It doesn't mean we didn't love you," Fiora added, not wanting to hurt her sister's feelings and yet compelled to speak the truth.

Fiora didn't know what would happen once they reached the city. She was confident her sister had a future with Grier, but her future with Jaxx was unreadable. This might be the only time they had to have this conversation.

Fiora placed her hands on Salena's shoulders, forcing her to meet her gaze. "And just like I'm not that girl, you aren't your old self either. We've changed. It's going to take time to find our new rhythm and get to know each other again. I hope we have that kind of time. We can't expect things just to be what they were, but that doesn't mean I don't love you or won't do everything I can think of to find Piera. You will always be my sister, and I will always have that connection to you even if it doesn't feel the same."

The heavy thud of footsteps came down the path. Grier appeared in dragon form. Jaxx made a series of low growls in his throat, and Grier answered him. Fiora had no idea what they were saying to each other.

"We will have that kind of time," Salena stated. "I'm not going to lose you again."

"I don't know if that's true," Fiora said. "I hope it is."

Salena leaned forward to hug her. "Sometimes I hate your honesty. I forgot how annoying it could be."

"And I hate it when you say things to try to make me feel better. I can never tell if you're lying or not," Fiora patted her sister's back a few times before ending the hug. She started toward Jaxx. A tiny headache formed, and she frowned. "Uh, Salena, make sure you pay attention to your dismount today. The ground is going to be uneven, and you don't want to break an ankle."

"Thanks for letting me know." Salena held up the pack she carried. "There is a handheld medic in here if we need it."

Grier reached to take the pack from his wife. She then climbed onto his back and held on to the base of his wings. Salena gave him a small tap.

Grier pushed up from the ground, beating his wings to lift them into the air. Fiora watched as Grier angled himself upward and flew through a canopy of leaves.

When they were alone, she turned her attention

to Jaxx. He dipped his head and crouched low to the ground to give her a way to climb on top of him. She drew her hand over the bumpy texture of his neck. The hard layer of flesh didn't mold to her fingers, not like when she touched his muscles.

Jaxx lifted his wing out of her way so she could walk under it. Fiora ran her fingers along the underside. His wing shook and twitched. He snorted a short blast of smoke.

"Did that tickle?" She asked, already guessing the answer.

He gave a small nod.

Fiora smiled, resisting the urge to do it again.

This was another of those moments she wanted to hold on to forever, like being naked in his arms.

When she touched his side, she felt the rise and fall of his breath. The rhythm calmed the tiny jump of fear in her chest as she took hold of the base of his wing and pulled herself onto his back. He rocked to the side to help her find her balance.

Fiora sat with her legs to one side before leaning over to straddle his back. One of the short spikes near the base of his tail poked her thigh. She fidgeted with her positioning, unsure of what would be best.

Fiora glanced up at the sky before burying her head in his back and holding on to his wings. She tightly closed her eyes. Jaxx slowly straightened. His wings moved, and she bit the inside of her mouth to keep from yelping. He shifted beneath her, his body undulating with each beat of his wings. She felt the moment they lifted from the ground.

Fiora turned her head to the side and peeked through narrow slits of her eyelids to see that they moved past the tree trunks into the branches. She gripped him tighter. She kept her head turned to keep from looking down as they went higher. Unlike Grier who had angled upward to fly through the tree-tops, Jaxx kept her parallel to the ground. Leaves hit her back and brushed over her skin before sliding past her as they broke free of the forest ceiling.

A sea of dark green leaves spread out before her, mimicking a strangely dancing carpet next to the green-blue sky. They led to the peaks and cliffs of distant mountains. The clouds drifted above them. If she ignored the fact that they were high above the ground, the view was almost serene.

Grier flew with Salena in the distance, circling in the air as if waiting for them to join them. Seeing him in flight caused her stomach to do a tiny flip of appre-hension, and she strengthened her grip on Jaxx. When her fingers began to feel numb, she forced them to ease up, worried that she might somehow injure him—which was probably ridiculous because his skin was like armor.

He hovered for a moment as if giving her time to adjust. When finally he moved to follow Grier, he took it slow and steady. The sound of the wind drowned out all else. Jaxx's body heat staved off the cooler temperature.

She watched her sister, seeing her outline against Grier's back. Salena stayed low, much like Fiora against Jaxx.

Never would she have predicted that one day she'd be riding on a dragon's back...or that she would be in love with that dragon.

Love.

That one thought caused her to relax. She loved Jaxx and trusted him.

Her legs loosened their tight grip. Jaxx began to fly a little faster. He stayed parallel to the ground, turning on a wide angle. She slowly pushed up from his back, still holding onto his wings. The treetops moved beneath her, blurring.

The wind whipped her hair back from her face. She felt the pressure of it along her torso, molding her clothing. The beauty of the scene was undeniable. She could see why Jaxx loved his planet so much. The cold air got to her, and she wasn't able to sit up for long.

Fiora leaned down against his body, pressing her breasts and stomach tight to soak in his heat. Riding on his back was nothing like dangling from talons. She much preferred this method.

They headed toward the distant mountains. Eventually, the tiniest outline of the watchtower appeared along the edge. Then hints of the Federation stronghold over Shelter City.

Fiora pushed up again to try to get a better look at the city below. Suddenly, a rush of emotions hit her. Jaxx had been right. Touching his dragon skin didn't stop the visions. She'd been so focused on flying that she had forgotten about the timelines.

The sky lit up with the orange glow of a fire seconds before a giant ball of flames appeared. Distant shouts filled her ears as the people below panicked in their futures. She tried to drop against Jaxx's back, but an explosive force of heat blasted her. She tried to hold on, but her hands were pried from his wings. Fiora screamed as she rolled through the air over his spiny tail. A sharp point sliced her arm when she tried to grab hold of him.

There was no time to think of the pain as she found herself launched over the forest. Her limbs flailed as she tried to grab hold of nothingness to stop her descent. Another scream ripped from her lungs as terror filled her. She saw Jaxx swooping above her and remembered what he'd said.

Fiora forced her shaking arms to the side. She plummeted toward the treetops. A wave of fire rolled over the top of them as the future visions overlaid the actual present. She closed her eyes as the flames came closer.

Please. Please. Plea—ah!

Her feet hit the canopy of leaves just as two vice-like grips formed on her biceps. Jaxx jerked her away from the trees, changing her trajectory. Her feet swung up over her head. They made contact with the underside of his jaw.

Jaxx's head snapped back, and he flipped in the air in a backward somersault. Fiora cried out in surprise as she was flung around with him. Her stomach fluttered in warning as nausea rose in her throat. He completed the rotation and steadied his flight pattern.

Fiora gasped for breath. She stretched her fingers but was only able to feel the air. Jaxx kept a tight grip on her arms as she dangled beneath him. The grip stopped the circulation in her arms, but at the moment she didn't care about her tingling hands. His flight was overly cautious as he slowly carried her toward a clearing.

The timelines became stronger. They were just as chaotic as the first time she'd flown by the city, but not as amplified without the boost the Federation scientists had injected into her. Screams echoed all around her. Balls of smoke and fire billowed into the air. The sky became dark, darker than should have been possible with the constant daylight of the planet. Ash hung thick in the atmosphere, choking her lungs and making it difficult to breathe.

Those in the middle of the city who were not lucky enough to instantly burn were suffocating in the aftermath. As the pain fanned out from the epicenter, some were able to escape only to starve in the woods. People turned on each other, killing in anger and fear. Others ate poisonous berries in hungry desperation, having navigated burnt forests. Yet others fell asleep in patches of yellow ferns, the spores drugging them into oblivious death.

One moment she felt like she was on fire, the next she ran through a forest, then she was back flying in the air, and then writhing in agony on the ground. She was stabbed, blasted, kicked off the side of a cliff. Yellow pollen tickled her nose seconds before she slit someone's throat from behind. The sensations washed over her, fighting for dominance.

Synapses fired in her brain. All of the sensations felt real, although at the same time only a few of them were from the present. She couldn't differentiate between them.

Something bounced against her heels. The skid of earth sounded as her feet were dragged over the ground. When her feet stopped, her ass dropped onto the uneven rock, followed by her back and head.

Jaxx released his hold on her arms, and she blinked in surprise to see he'd ended their flight. For a second, the sky cleared of fire and she watched Grier fly over her. Particles of ash followed him, falling like black snow.

"Fiora?"

Jaxx appeared over her, and he took hold of her face. The ash disappeared the second he made contact.

"Fiora?" Jaxx repeated. "Look at me."

She tried to lift her hands to cover his, but she couldn't move her arms.

"I don't know what happened. I'm sorry, I tried to take it slow for you." Jaxx continued to hold her face.

"Fiora?" Salena yelled. A thud sounded as Grier landed.

"She's hurt. I need the handheld medic. She cut her arm on my tail," Jaxx answered.

"I'm com—" Salena jumped from Grier's back, only to cry out in pain. "Blast it all, my ankle! I think I broke it."

"Selen—?" Grier started to ask.

"Help Fiora," Salena ordered, her voice strained. "Jaxx needs the handheld."

Fiora heard Grier digging in the pack.

"Got it," Grier said. "Catch."

Jaxx released her face to catch the unit. Ash began to fall all around her at the lack of contact. Fiora closed her eyes and coughed as it landed on her lips. The slightly metallic taste flavored her mouth, and she tried not to breathe.

Jaxx grabbed her arm, and the ash-fall stopped. When she opened her eyes, he was leaning over her, healing a cut on her arm.

"I'm so sorry," he whispered.

"It's not your fault," she answered. "I shouldn't have sat up. I should have been ready for the time-lines. They caught me off guard. I knew better."

"Oo-ow," Salena moaned. "Yeah, definitely broken."

"I tried to warn you to watch your dismount," Fiora said.

"I wasn't thinking about me. I was preoccupied with the fact you decided to skydive off Jaxx," Salena countered, sounding grouchy.

"Not on purpose," Fiora answered. The pain eased from her arm, not that she'd been focusing on it.

"Give me the medic," Grier said to his cousin.

Jaxx tossed the handheld over to him.

"Help me up." Fiora grabbed hold of Jaxx's arm. He pulled her to sitting. She felt a little dizzy.

"Better?" Grier asked Salena, holding the handheld medic to her ankle.

"A little sore, but yeah, better," Salena answered. "Thank you."

"You're bleeding," Jaxx said, gesturing to her nose.

Fiora swiped at her nose. "It'll go away."

"Do you want to tell me what you saw?" Jaxx asked. His touch kept the information from replaying in her mind and becoming physically painful.

"An explosion starts in the center of town," Fiora said. "It either spreads or there are more explosions, catching the forest on fire. Ash chokes the city, killing more people than the explosions.

Citizens turn on each other. In the aftermath, lawlessness spills toward the shifter settlements. Some people starve, others die in various horrific ways."

"Did you see how we stop it?" Grier asked.

"No. I see the effects, not the cause." Fiora placed her hand over Jaxx's. "You'll need to take me into the city. We can talk to that cyborg Salena was talking about."

"Yevgen," Salena supplied. "He'll know of any threats. If you find the right targets to read, you will find which timelines to follow."

"My thoughts exactly," Fiora said. "If we can find who or what starts this, maybe we can stop it."

"You're sure we can trust him?" Jaxx asked.

Fiora understood his concern. Cyborgs were both man and computer. It was sometimes difficult to tell how much was human and how much was programming. Robots followed a set of protocols and programs, some learning programs, but at their base core they had a primary function. Humans were unprecdictable. Combine human emotion with a robotic function, and you could get a dangerous combination.

Salena nodded. "Yes. I trust him. He helped us find Fiora. However, I'll warn you that I can't force him to speak the truth. The machine in him is able to override the compulsion in the man."

"You're in no condition to walk," Grier said to his wife. "You should stay in the—"

"My sister is not going in there alone," Salena insisted.

"She won't be alone. I'll be there," Jaxx said.

"Take me or I follow you after you leave," Salena warned. "Your choice. Yevgen knows me. I can get him to trust you."

"But your foot..." Grier began.

"I've seen glimpses of your future," Fiora said. "I know you both make it out alive today."

Grier seemed to relax at the news.

"Maybe you stay here and we'll go see Yevgen," Salena said. "Since you can't see your future. Just to be safe."

"Take me or I follow," Fiora answered, arching a brow as she repeated Salena's threat.

"Fair enough." Her sister stood and rocked on her ankle. She reached for the handheld and typed in a program before pressing the device to her neck.

"What did you do?" Grier asked, checking the screen.

"Something to dull the pain. I promise to rest my ankle when this is over," Salena said.

"A neuro-blocker?" Grier frowned. "Is this safe?"

Fiora pulled Jaxx's hand away from her as she concentrated on her sister. "She'll be in pain later once they wear off. You should get her to a medical booth as soon as you can."

Jaxx took her hand to stop Salena's timeline flow. "Can you stand?"

Fiora nodded. "I'm a little dizzy from the flight, but that will pass."

Grier pulled the clothes out of the pack and began to dress. He paused long enough to toss a pair of pants at Jaxx.

"There is a stockpile of cloaks we can use to disguise our clothing. We'll pick them up from a cache on the way into the city," Jaxx said.

Fiora let go of Jaxx so he could dress. She walked along a rocky path. The Federation building was on the other side of a valley. She was too far from the cliffside to see Shelter City. A glow emanated from the settlement below. She lifted her hands to each side and felt the tickle of ash against her skin. The screams filled her mind, and she knew she was the only one who could hear them crying out for help. She listened to their torment as it wrenched her insides.

Fiora wanted to save them, just as she wanted to

throw herself off the side of the cliff to make the pain stop.

"It's not too late to turn back," Jaxx said behind her.

Fiora dropped her hands. "Yes. It is."

14

Fiora clung to Jaxx's arm as they walked through the city. When she touched him, she didn't feel even the slightest hum of a timeline—and there were many timelines to follow. She couldn't remember ever being able to be around so many people without wanting to cry out in pain. The visions should have been overwhelming.

Mud caked a few of her locks, causing them to hang heavy. A dirty piece fell close to her cheek. The cloak she wore had a musty smell as if stored damp. The material was patched together, and even that didn't hide the worn spots. Salena wore a similar one as she walked ahead of them with Grier. The men had darker jackets worn thin at the elbows and cuffs.

With Jaxx at her side she could look at faces,

brush against arms and not pick up a hint of tragedy or joy. It was nothingness and she loved it, especially when she knew what letting go of Jaxx could mean. It was with childlike wonder that she moved through the thickening crowd—so many people with secrets being kept from her. It was exhilarating and terrifying at the same time.

An unshaven face covered in dots of mud looked as compelling as any fine painting, more so because it moved, and breathed, and frowned at her staring. There was not much laughter in the streets, but the shouts of city dwellers and the scolding of a father to his child rose in a chorus of the present time. There was not picking apart what was real and what would be real someday. It was all now.

Glorious, perfect now.

Well, maybe not *glorious*. She needed to rein in her excitement over walking through a crowd unhampered by visions for the first time and remember why they were there in the first place.

Her feet trampled through mud, but she didn't care. Mud reminded her of the clay pits from childhood, and she enjoyed the clomp and sticky pull of it against her boots. The one thing she could do without was the smell. The crush of bodies over a long period had marked the area with an underlying stench that even a breeze did little to resolve.

Jaxx kept to the streets, away from the crowded sidewalks. Warped boards created the walkways but were hardly kept clean.

Decay and rust ran as a theme through the structures. Patched metal repairs were held in place with corroded bolts and swipes of quick-drying polymers covered holes. The buildings were tethered together with rope. She couldn't imagine any place more opposite to the Federation stronghold with its pristine and sterile walls.

Jaxx kept glancing in her direction as if gauging her response to everything. His serious expression drew her back from the carnival of the city sights to the reality of why they were here. She clung to his hand, not wanting to risk an apocalyptic vision while so many people were curiously watching them.

Suddenly a loud whack reverberated from between two of the dilapidated buildings, and a man stumbled in front of them. He tripped on the warped boards and slid across the muddy street. Jaxx swept Fiora into his chest and jumped out of the way.

The man stopped sliding. He jumped up with a growl and charged back between the buildings. Fiora tried to watch, but Jaxx pulled her away from the fight.

Salena stared back at them. Fiora nodded and mouthed that she was unharmed.

As they walked down the street another fight, by all evidence unrelated to the first, broke out between a merchant and customer. Shouts escalated to into a brawl within seconds. The customer knocked over a stall of metal trinkets. Onlookers began to cheer, though it hardly seemed they were invested in who won. A woman ushered her child past the throng as if such were an everyday occurrence.

"Meat. Less than a week old," a woman yelled, not sounding very enthusiastic as she pointed toward her questionable wares. "We accept trade."

Jaxx escorted her at hurried pace as they turned through a narrow marketplace.

"Half price love," a gruff voice yelled. The man wore a dirty yellow shirt with holes in it. "One stone will get you a date with a pleasure droid."

"Half price for half a droid," another man teased, mimicking Yellow-shirt's voice. "Half a stone will get you his hand."

"He'd have to pay me for his hand," a woman cackled. She jumped up and wiggled her hips, grinning a toothless grin. "Fifty-five stones!"

Yellow Shirt dismissed her with a wave. "Even the mites won't go under those diseased skirts."

Toothless pursed her lips to mimic a kiss and then smacked her backside.

"That's the man who stole our food simulators," Jaxx said, nodding toward Yellow-shirt. "We're still trying to find where he hides them."

She tried to pull her hand from his, but he held on tighter.

"You don't have to," he said. "We'll find another way."

"I'm here to help these people. Let me help." Fiora slipped her hand from Jaxx's and stared at the grotesque merchant.

Ash started to fall, and all the people around her looked up at the sky in shock seconds before debris began to rain down upon them. She pushed past the dominant vision to peek beneath. She saw Yellow Shirt sneaking out of his house, and a vision of him in black ghosted over his currently lewd gestures toward the toothless woman.

Fiora followed him with her mind, trying to pick out his secret. She watched him pull a piece of the warped walking boards behind his shop where he kept a stash of goods.

"What are you looking at?" Yellow Shirt yelled.

The present pulled her from the future. "What's wrong with her? She got the radiation sickness?"

Fiora touched her nose. It was bleeding. Blocking the death event made it harder to concentrate on the information she sought. Jaxx grabbed her hand.

"We don't want no sick here," the toothless woman added.

"Get her out of here," another man yelled, his gruff voice indicating he was ready to make it happen if Jaxx didn't.

Jaxx quickly led her from the marketplace. They came out on a new street.

"I hate using you for visions. I know how much it hurts you," he said.

"I appreciate that, but if I'm going to have visions —*and I am*—they might as well be useful," she answered.

"What did you see?" he asked, as they continued to walk after Grier and her sister.

"I think your missing simulators are behind his shop, under the walkway, inside a large pit dug into the dirt. It's where he stores all his goods," Fiora answered. "It's all I saw."

"Thank you." Jaxx nodded. "That's more than we had a few moments ago."

The roads were unmarked, and after several

more turns, Fiora knew she'd be lost in the city if left on her own. She held tighter to Jaxx's hand.

"What is it?" he asked, concerned.

"I'm lost," she answered. "I was too busy watching people that I forgot to pay attention to where we were going."

"We're almost there," he assured her. "I won't leave your side. I've stared at this city from above until I memorized its patterns. We're not lost."

Salena glanced back to make sure they were still following before she and Grier turned a corner and moved out of sight

A redheaded woman shoved a piece of dirty parchment into her hands. "Join us in the fight against—"

"Back off," Jaxx warned.

"Don't fall victim to fear," the redhead said. Her stained gown had been patched and appeared clean. Her hair was pulled to the top of her head, twisted around the crown to keep the locks out of the way. "We must fight if we want our freedom from the tyranny of Shelter City."

Fiora pulled her hand from Jaxx. She unfolded the paper to read it before she thoroughly considered the action. The ash began to fall. She tried to ignore it.

The redhead's timeline flashed, but the instant burst was replaced with stronger images. The woman didn't move. Her skin began to smoke and peel away from her face as if hit by a laser. Screams echoed but the redhead only stared at her with sad eyes.

Jaxx took Fiora's hand and the vision instantly disappeared.

"You all right?" the redhead asked, frowning as she stared at Fiora's nose. The blood must have smeared on her face. It wasn't the first time she'd caught someone staring at her nose. She reached to cover it.

"She's fine," Jaxx answered.

"No," Fiora said, forced to tell the truth.

The redhead's eyes narrowed. She sprang into action, attacking Jaxx as she ripped Fiora away from him. She shoved the heel of her hand toward his jaw. Jaxx's head snapped back at the sudden assault but he only lifted his hands in defense, choosing not to hurt the woman.

"Run!" the redhead yelled.

Fiora stood with her arms to the side as a rush of agony overcame her. Fire rolled down the street, causing buildings to explode and people to cry out in pain. Panic ensued as people rushed past her like ghosts over the present. The fire came closer, so hot she could feel it bubbling her flesh.

The redhead tried to pull Fiora's arm to get her to safety. Fiora jerked away from her.

"Stop." Fiora's voice was weak. She began to shake. "Jaxx. I can't see you."

Jaxx rushed to Fiora. He put his hands on Fiora's face, ending the vision. A rush of cool hit her body and she gasped for breath.

"Look at me. You're all right. I'm here," Jaxx said.

Tears rolled down her cheeks. "There's so much. We have to stop it."

"I know, love, I know," Jaxx soothed. He ran his thumb under her bleeding nose.

"What's wrong with her?" the redhead asked, eyeing them warily.

"Nothing," Jaxx answered.

"There's so much," Fiora repeated. "These people shouldn't be here. We have to make it stop."

"Shh, we will, my love, we will," Jaxx assured her. "We can't talk about it here."

"Jaxx, we have to go," Grier appeared at their side. "We're starting to draw the attention of sweeper borgs."

The redhead stared at Fiora a moment, before

finally judging that Jaxx meant her no harm. "I thought you were hurting her."

It wasn't much of an apology. Jaxx ignored the woman as he wrapped an arm around Fiora to guide her steps.

"We have to walk," Jaxx urged.

"I know," Fiora whispered, still teary as the remnants of grief rolled through her. Her legs felt wobbly.

Fiora blinked in surprise as the redhead touched her arm. "You're not from Shelter City, are you?"

"No," Fiora answered. "I was being held by the Federation. I escaped, and now we're trying to—"

Jaxx wrapped his hand gently over her mouth and walked faster. "I'm sorry about this."

"Enough said. I'll handle the sweepers," the woman stated. "Those buckets of rust are stupider than a pile of Federation rubble."

Jaxx removed his hand, and Fiora glanced back to see the redhead kicking a metal wall before taking off down an alley. The sound of banging followed the woman.

"What are sweeper borgs?" Fiora asked. Two men ran after the redhead, following the ruckus she made.

"The Federation reconditioned old rubbish

collecting droids into cheap hitmen to police the citizens of Shelter City," Jaxx said. "They're not working with the smartest processors, but they are dangerous if engaged."

Grier and Salena waited near a narrow opening between two structures. Seeing them Salena slipped between the buildings. Grier and Jaxx barely fit as they all had to turn sideways to pass through. They turned a corner, still sideways as they moved into a shaded inlet.

"Careful," Salena said. "There's a step up."

They turned yet another corner. Fiora held Jaxx's arm, letting him guide her in the dark. A thud sounded, and suddenly there was a blue light coming from behind an old board that acted as a door. Exterior building walls made the secret nook, and sheets of metal had been laid over the top to create a hidden room of odd angles and mismatched colors.

"Yevgen, are you here?" Salena called. "It's Salena. I came before with Princess Payton."

Fiora was the last to step into the strange space. The blue glow came from a wall of monitors, all in various states of grainy dilapidation. Sounds seemed to come from all of them, creating a low murmur of tones that acted more like white noise. They appeared to be surveillance of the city, each one showing a different area. The largest, clearest monitor showed the outside of the Federation building and political housing on top of the cliff.

"Yevgen?" Salena called again, looking upward. Her gaze followed along metal tracks in the ceiling.

Suddenly the sound of rolling metal came from behind the monitors. A legless man sat in a sling that hung from the ceiling. It rolled along the tracks. His arms hung out of the side of the sling. When he looked at her, she remembered Yevgen wasn't a man at all. He was a cyborg. His mechanical eyes focused in on her like a security camera. Fiora saw them appear on one of the monitors as his eyes zoomed in on them.

"Future queen of the dragons," Yevgen said, bowing his head. Salena's face became focused on the screen and the image of starbursts appeared around her like fireworks. His voice wasn't what Fiora would have expected. It had a pleasant quality to it. "An honor to see you again so soon."

"It is good to see you, Yevgen," Salena said.

"Prince Grier. Prince Jaxx," Yevgen said to the men in turn, their faces appearing with less fanfare on the monitor. "I have seen you both several times sneaking through our city."

Yevgen's gaze then settled on Fiora. A monitor

behind him flickered, and a poster of her appeared on the screen. The image zoomed in to the scar on her forehead.

"I am pleased to see you have found freedom, Lady Fiora," Yevgen said. "I wondered if we would ever meet. I have been picking up communications about you for some time."

"Yevgen is the one who told us they were bringing off-world dignitaries into the facility for that big gala," Salena said. "It gave us our opening to get to you."

"Yes. They were bringing generals and captains who needed convincing of Shelter City's relevance. They tried to hide the reason for their landings with fake planetary clearance codes, but they referenced a soothsayer in their communications," Yevgen added. "Thankfully, your escape did not help secure their galactic position. The general was very disappointed to lose you."

"Then I owe you my thanks," Fiora said.

Yevgen's eyes dilated. He focused in on her as if registering her physiological reactions. The monitor showed a recording of Grier running them off the side of the cliff during their escape from the stronghold. As they fell, a large white cat had jumped from the trees only to drag a fallen soldier into the brush.

The image lasted several seconds before it returned to the present. Her scar became a highlighted line for a brief moment as if he logged the anomaly into his database.

"But I cannot say I would have recommended a level-one prisoner of the Federation's return to the city," Yevgen continued. "The general was not happy to lose such a prized possession."

Yevgen glanced to where Jaxx held her hand.

"It would seem another has taken possession," the cyborg said.

Fiora followed his gaze down. She wasn't sure she liked being called a possession but didn't correct him. They needed his help.

"Or perhaps you have taken possession of him?" Yevgen mused. "Another dragon prince tamed?"

"Yes," Jaxx said. "Without hesitation or regret."

"Any others with you?" Yevgen slid to look behind them. His eyes filled with electricity at the question.

"No, no others," Salena said.

"This place is getting crowded." A woman appeared from behind the monitors. She wore a black shirt with cross laces down the front from neck to stomach and tight pants with sleek boots.

"Payton!" Salena went to the cat-shifter princess and hugged her. "What are you doing here?"

"We're missing a runner," Payton said. She reminded Fiora of Grace. It wasn't so much how she looked, but the way she carried herself. It couldn't be easy being the rare female shifters on a male-dominated world. "He didn't show to pick up his load of food supplies. I'm trying to find him."

Yevgen's sling turned and rolled closer to the monitors. He pointed to a screen to show Yellow Shirt. "He was looking into the man who stole the food simulators."

"We saw him. Is that your runner or the thief?" Grier asked.

"Thief," Yevgen said.

"Fiora might have a lead on the simulators," Jaxx put forth. "Behind his stop, buried beneath the walkway."

"How...?" Payton began. "Never mind. That's amazing. Thank you."

The monitor blipped, and Yevgen continued, "This is our missing runner. I fear he is dead. People who go missing in Shelter City tend not to be found."

A familiar face appeared on the screen.

"That's Brogan," Fiora said.

"You know him? Does the Federation have him?" Yevgen asked.

"No. He's on his way to the northern mountains with his sister," Fiora said. "Brogan is safe."

"Dulla escaped her husband." Yevgen gave a small smile. "Brogan is taking her to the mountains where they may live in peace. That is an ending I enjoy. There are not many happy endings to the stories of Shelter City. You know for sure that they are safe?"

Fiora bit her lip and didn't want to answer. "Brogan and the two babies will live. Dulla will die soon in childbirth."

Yevgen's smile faded. "You say that with such certainty. The rumors about your future sight are true."

"They are," Fiora said.

"Death of a mother. That sounds more like a story from Shelter City." Yevgen sighed and nodded.

"Fiora, I'm Payton." The princess held up her hand. "I was pleased to see you escape the stronghold."

"Was that you dragging the guard when we jumped off the cliff?" Fiora asked, gesturing to the monitor.

"It was." Payton gave a small laugh as Fiora's eyes

widened. "Don't worry. I didn't eat him or anything. He woke up hours later with a nasty headache. I thought it best to give you all as far of a head start as possible. We didn't need him alerting the others."

"Thank you for helping me," Fiora said.

"You're welcome. I'm happy you're free but I have to agree with Yevgen. You shouldn't be in the city," Payton said. "Not after what it took to break you out of prison. If they catch you again, we might never get another chance."

"I have to be here," Fiora answered. She couldn't turn away from so many future deaths. "I wish I didn't, but I do."

"As much as I want to believe it's because of my winning personality that you're all here, I have to believe you're looking for information." Yevgen turned to the monitors. "What are you searching for, and what do you have to trade for it? Nothing in Shelter City is free. The future dragon queen already owes me a favor, so it will have to be something else."

"How about life?" Jaxx asked.

Yevgen spun around on his sling and slid away from them. The monitor lights went from blue to yellow and began to flash a countdown sequence. "Threats don't work on me."

"Calm yourself," Grier stated.

"It's not a threat," Salena assured him.

"I wasn't threatening your life," Jaxx said.

"I saw a bleak future. A great explosion is going to hit the city," Fiora explained. She looked at the monitors wondering if this was the beginning of what she saw. "We're here to stop it. We don't want to hurt anyone."

The countdown on the monitors stopped and the yellow faded to blue. She took a deep breath. It was not going to be what caused the explosion.

"And you think it starts here?" Yevgen frowned. "My system is—"

"No." Fiora kept hold of Jaxx, knowing she would have to let go of him again soon. "I only see the event, not the cause. I need you to show me who might be most likely to blow up the city. I need to narrow down who I'm reading."

"Are there any troublemakers you think might do something like this?" Salena asked Yevgen.

"Besides the usual?" Yevgen slowly slid back toward them. "Let me check my database."

"When is this supposed to happen?" Payton asked Fiora.

"I'm not sure. There's so much information. We're here trying to narrow it down." Fiora felt emotionally drained from the moments she'd already seen.

"Has anyone been vocal about ending the city?" Jaxx asked.

"That narrows it down to about three-fourths of the population," Yevgen answered. "And I guarantee the rest of them think it."

"Anyone who seems capable of killing?" Salena asked.

"Everyone is capable in the right circumstance," Fiora answered.

"You're a dark one, aren't you?" Yevgen chuckled. "I like you."

"I've been warned that negativity is a side effect of seeing so much." Fiora glanced at Jaxx. "Though I don't feel that way when I'm with you. Your presence eases me. You give me hope."

"Ah, that's so sweet," Payton told her friend, teasing him a little. "I'm happy for you, Jaxx."

"Any threats?" Salena prompted, trying to get the conversation back on track. Fiora realized that Yevgen's resistance to answering her sister was frustrating Salena greatly.

"And you're always in a hurry," Yevgen told Salena, arching a brow toward his screen. "I've been monitoring a lot of activity. I'm not sure any of it is what you're looking for." He placed his hands on a small console beside the monitors. A series of paused videos appeared on the screens to show faces.

"Who is that woman?" Fiora pointed at the redhead that had tried to rescue her from Jaxx.

"Justina," Payton said.

"She tends to have her ear to the mud in this town. I've been trying to recruit her, but you wouldn't believe how difficult it is to lure women into my fortress," Yevgen answered. "She's been warning citizens about a thief that's terrorizing the Federation and threatening to pull their wrath down on the city. I've heard rumors but am close to concluding that it is only a local myth at this point."

"It's not her. I had a vision of her face melting off during the blast." Fiora tried not to picture the images she referenced. "But maybe the thief caused this."

"I agree. Justina doesn't come off as a killer. She's more likely to get herself killed with that mouth of hers." Payton frowned. "Who else?"

Fiora pointed toward the man in the yellow shirt. "It's not him, and it's not any of the vendors I saw in the marketplace. They'll be hit by falling debris from an explosion."

Justina, Yellow Shirt, and a few more images

disappeared from the batch as he took her at her word.

"How do you find all this footage?" Fiora asked. "I didn't see any cameras or recording droids in the area."

"Yevgen knows everything that happens in the city," Payton patted his arm. "He's my go-to guy."

"Careful with the flattery, princess. You already know I'm in love with you," Yevgen said.

Payton laughed. "You say that to all the single women."

"True." Yevgen nodded. "I do fall for a pretty face."

The screens flashed to show a variety of women before flickering back to their original images.

"Who else is capable?" Salena asked.

"This man is accident prone," Yevgen said. A young man with torn clothing began moving on a monitor. He leaned against a building and it instantly began to shake. Within moments it collapsed, falling into the building next to it, only to knock the second building over, and then a third and fourth. The scene changed to show the same man tripping on a warped plank to launch a woman with a fruit basket into the mud. Next it showed the man reaching for a torch without looking directly at it and knocking the flames over to set a tent on fire. "If anyone was to accidentally stumble onto an antiquated nuclear reactor to destroy a city, this is the Cysgodian who'll do it."

"I'm not sure clumsy equals destroyer of worlds," Grier said.

"We should focus on intentional acts." Fiora didn't want to create more suspects. She needed to narrow them down. "We have to start somewhere. If we start including accidents, then I'll be forced to read everyone in the city."

Fiora leaned against Jaxx and closed her eyes. She felt the steady heartbeat in his chest. She wished the world would disappear and leave her alone with him. That's all she wanted—a simple life away from crowds.

"What about those Cysgodians we came across in the forest? The ones who want to," Salena frowned and glanced at Grier, "um, to dine on shifters."

"Ew." Fiora wrinkled her nose in disgust and tried not to gag.

"Raimon, Partha, Bharath, X," Yevgen said.

"Yes, those men," Salena turned toward Fiora and added, "They attacked us in the forest so we know they venture out of the city. Maybe they're trying to plan an escape—or *something*—and want to use the explosion as a distraction."

"I am watching them," Yevgen said. "They lack the focus to be considered a serious large-scale threat. They're harmless unless you're alone with them."

"What about the Doyen?" Payton gestured toward the picture of a man in a black cloak.

Fiora frowned and leaned closer. "He looks familiar. I think I've seen him in some of the timelines."

Her arms stretched behind her as Jaxx kept a hold of her hand.

"It's like looking at a blurry dream. I can just about see it, but..." Fiora frowned.

"Play the recordings you have of him," Salena suggested. "It might help focus the timeline for her."

The recording showed the man standing in front of what sounded like a mob of people, though they were not part of the image.

"The key is not the blue sun." Rage dripped from Doyen's words. "That is merely a distraction they hang in the sky to hide the truth. If anything, it's hurting us with its poison. We are dying, our lives shortened, our children's future corrupted and stolen by the greed of others. The Federation caused the virus and then pretended to save us as they took over our dead planet. They moved us here, into this valley of disrepair. Now, why is it our shifter neighbors live five times—no, *ten times* longer than a Cysgodian man? They breathe the same air, and they feel the same sun, yet they do not suffer the loss that we do. They eat while we starve. They fly free as we are trapped in this city of rust."

The sound cut out but the image of Doyen kept going, thrusting his arms the air in a silenced yell.

"Fiora? Does he sound familiar?" Salena asked.

"Yes?" Fiora still couldn't exactly place him.

"...survival of our people depends upon action." Doyen's voice returned with the sound of cheers distorting his words. It became clear by the shouts that the crowd were his followers. "No one wants to go to war, but if we do not fight, we will die. They delivered us to this battle!"

"I don't know—" Fiora began.

"Shh, watch," Salena nodded toward the screen.

"If it's not the sun, if it's not the air, if it's not the dirt we all walk on, what is it? What is the key?" Doyen held up both arms as if to make himself appear taller.

"Blood," the crowd shouted.

"It's in the blood!" Doyen incited his followers as he leaned his head back to yell his hate.

"Blood, blood, blood," the crowd chanted.

Yevgen stopped the recording. Doyen was frozen with his fist pumped into the air.

"I'd say we have a strong contender," Grier said, breaking the silence in the room.

"Fiora?" Jaxx asked.

"I think someone harboring that much hatred in his heart would definitely be on the list of possibilities." Fiora didn't need to see the man's future to know it would not end well for a lot of people. "I have never come across an extremist group like that who were destined for a happy ending. Usually it's mass murder, mass suicide, or both."

"Yevgen, where can we find Doyen?" Payton asked.

"I'll see what I can discover," Yevgen's screens began blinking through cityscapes.

"Can you show me an aerial view of the city? From the direction of the watchtower?" Fiora asked.

The images she requested appeared. She studied it before pointing to a central area near the cliff beneath the Federation building. "Which one of these people we've talked about is in this area? When we were in the sky, I think the blast started somewhere around here."

"Doyen," Yevgen and Payton answered at the same time.

"Sounds like we have a winner," Salena said.

"I don't like the idea of you going near that man," Jaxx said.

"I agree," Grier added.

"I would also have to advise against it," Yevgen said, still searching the city. "Doyen is surrounded by loyal followers. By their doctrine, they will kill any shifter on sight and do not have kind regard for women."

"I don't have to be face to face with him. Just get me in the vicinity. The closer I am, the easier it is to focus, but I shouldn't have to talk to him." Fiora closed her eyes and took a deep breath. Dread rolled through her.

"What is it?" Salena touched her arm.

"I'm scared. I know I'm not going to like what I see." Fiora opened her eyes to find they were all staring at her.

Jaxx pulled her against his chest and wrapped her in his arms. "At any time you say the word, I'll fly you out of here."

"We can try to find another way," Grier said.

"Whatever you need," Salena added.

Payton and Yevgen stayed quiet.

It was tempting, oh-so-tempting.

For a second, she let herself have the fantasy of running away.

Then she remembered falling, and that one memory tightened her stomach and brought her back to the anxiety of the present.

She let Jaxx hold her a few seconds longer before pulling away from his chest to face everyone. "This thing that I can do. I know Salena calls it a gift. I've often called it a curse. But whatever it is, for the first time in my life, I get to decide how to use it." She looked up at Jaxx. "I can't thank you enough for that."

Jaxx touched her cheek. "I love you. Whatever you decide, I support you."

She placed her hand over his. "If I can choose to do one good thing with my life, then I can think of nothing more important than trying to save all these people. If I don't try then how can I live with myself? There has to be a reason I am the way I am. Maybe this is that reason. Fates are drawn out in timelines I see. They're hard to change but they can change. This has to be my fate. Maybe, if I could have seen my own timeline, I would have changed something and missed this opportunity."

Fiora moved her hand to Jaxx's cheek.

"I might have missed you," she whispered, not caring that everyone watched them. This was one truth she wasn't embarrassed to say. "I love you, Jaxx."

He kissed her lightly. "We're going to get through this. Together."

"He's outside the eatery near the south cliffside," Yevgen said.

"I know where that is. It's near the blast zone you mentioned." Payton patted Yevgen on the shoulder. "I'll show them and come back to finish our discussion."

"Until then, sweet princess," Yevgen said.

Payton winked at him. To Fiora, she said, "You're in charge. You tell me when you're ready."

"Now," Fiora answered. "The sooner we get started, the sooner we'll be done."

"What if it isn't Doyen?" Salena asked.

"Then come back and we'll search for the next target." Yevgen pointed to the space behind the monitors. "I'll pull out the extra cots. It'll be just like an overnight party."

15

THE LAST PLACE JAXX WANTED TO TAKE FIORA was deeper into Shelter City. It took everything in him not to let the dragon take over and fly her away. He wanted to protect her from the evil she was sure to see in a man like Doyen's head. Each time she read a future, he saw the emotional toll it took on her. He saw the dullness fill her eyes, watched as she unconsciously rubbed her temple and the back of her neck, and the smear of blood staining her skin from her nosebleeds.

Payton's guidance took them through the city toward the cliffside under the Federation building. The cat-shifter princess moved as if she belonged in the city streets. She acted like the locals, navigating with ease, never hesitating, not making eye contact for too long.

"How much time does she spend here?" Fiora walked next to Jaxx. Grier and Salena followed behind them, and Payton took the lead several paces ahead. The smaller groups would draw less notice, and if one stumbled into trouble, two others could help.

"Who? Payton?" Jaxx gave a small laugh, trying to keep the mood as light as possible for Fiora. He didn't want her picking up on his worry. She had enough of her own. "Probably more than she should."

"She appears as if she is extremely familiar with the city," Fiora added.

"Her father commands the Var armies. He's all about keeping his little girl safe. He would hate it if he knew she snuck into the city," Jaxx said, thinking of Prince Falke of the Var.

"I have the distinct impression that none of the shifter elders would like the fact any of us are here, except maybe your parents. Well, maybe not like, but not hate," she answered.

"True." Jaxx scanned the crowd for threats. For the most part, it was city business as usual.

A father—at least he hoped it was a father figure —dragged two children behind him on a small cart.

The small boy cried and sniffled. The older girl looked annoyed with him. Neither seemed in danger.

Fiora must have noticed them as well because she pulled her hand from his. He glanced down, seeing her staring at the cart. Her eyes widened, and she turned her head away from them, gasping for breath.

Jaxx instantly grabbed her hand to stop it. "Maybe don't look at things until we're done with Doyen."

He wanted to say, *Stop letting go of me if it's going to cause you pain. I will gladly hold you forever.*

"Rocks," she whispered. "The explosion causes the rocks to fall here. Just when I saw all the ways these people die..." She took a deep, shaky breath. "Explosion, fire, ash, murder, poisoning, starvation, and now a rockfall caused by the blast. Jaxx, I have to stop this from happening. I *have* to, but what if I fail? What if I can't do it? What if I can't find the cause?"

"*We* have to. You are not in this alone, and this does not fall only on your head to solve. We are in this together." He pulled her closer to him and hated the way her shoulders trembled.

What they were doing went against every dragon instinct he had. For that matter, it went against his instincts as a man too. But Fiora was a strong woman, and he owed it to her not to dishonor that strength by ignoring her wishes.

"I love you, Fiora," Jaxx whispered. "More than anything I have ever loved in my life."

She glanced up at him and the shaking stopped. "And I love you."

"We should mate," he said before the thought fully formed in his brain.

Jaxx glanced around. This was not the most romantic place for such a proposal—in the middle of a Federation city on the way to read the future of a psychopathic murderer.

"Here?" She gave him a quizzical expression. "You want to have sex here, now? I guess—"

"Mate, marry me, wed," he corrected.

"Oh," Fiora laughed. "For a second I thought you meant... Well, actually, if we could work out the logistics of it, I'd say yes. I'll always say yes to the proposal of sex with you but I'm fairly sure you know that."

Jaxx knew she couldn't help her blunt honesty, but he didn't mind it. There should only be honesty between them.

"Everything all right?" Salena joined them, worried. "Why have you stopped?"

"Jaxx and I are going to be married," Fiora said,

smiling. She hadn't given him a direct answer until that moment.

"I figured as much. But why are you discussing that now?" Salena asked. "It's not like you can do this now. Jaxx, I thought Grace had your marriage crystal."

"She does," Jaxx said. "But just like I don't need a crystal to tell me who I am meant to be with, I don't need its permission to marry my heart."

"Agreed, but maybe it can be discussed later?" Salena insisted. "I don't want to be here any longer than we have to."

"Life is short and things need to be said," Fiora told her sister. "What if I don't come back from this? Of course we want to know where we stand with each other before going into danger." She then glanced at Jaxx. "If I don't come back from this, I want you to be happy and never blame yourself for anything that—"

"Salena is right," Jaxx cut her off. "We should focus on the task at hand. I'm not losing you today so there is no reason to discuss that."

What had he just been thinking about her honesty? This was not something he wanted to hear or even consider as a possibility. Once a dragon chose his mate, there was no one else for him. If he lost her, he would spend the rest of his life pining for his lost heart. He'd seen dragon-shifters who had fallen to such a horrible fate. They were strange creatures, broken and sad, waiting for a death that took it's time coming. When the planet had been at war—shifters against shifters—they were often the ones to volunteer for the most dangerous missions as if they hoped the gods would end their suffering.

"What is it?" Fiora asked. "What are you thinking?"

"It's not important right now," Jaxx answered.

"Wh—?" Salena began to ask him something and he held up his hand to stop her. He did not want to be forced into putting his worries on Fiora. Salena nodded and moved to rejoin Grier.

"I don't like you being here," he said when Fiora continued to stare at him.

"I understand. I don't like you being in danger either." She began walking toward where they had last seen Payton. "Any idea where she went?"

Jaxx glanced down toward soft impressions in the street that revealed where Payton had walked. He knew her stride and could pick the footprints out of the many. "This way."

His skin tingled with the threat of a shift. The dragon wanted to come out but the man held it back.

He searched each face they passed for signs of danger. For the most part, they were ignored, but there were a few who stared a little too long and it made him uncomfortable.

The pattern in the ground became distorted by heavy foot traffic. He searched for Payton in the crowd. A couple of beat-up sweeper borgs marched past with weapons. Old skin grafts had peeled away to leave a mechanical skeleton exposed. With each step one of them rattled lightly as if their parts weren't completely bolted together. Thankfully, they didn't stop in their progress.

"There," Fiora whispered.

Jaxx followed her gaze to a row of faded cloths drying in the breeze at the end of the street. The sound of flapping material became distinct against the noise of the city. The sweeper borgs continued on their way.

As material blew aside, he caught a glimpse of Payton watching them from beside the rocky cliff. She'd hidden behind a wide piece of cloth to wait for them to catch up. When he met her gaze, she waved them to join her.

Jaxx escorted Fiora past a corner building to where the street crossed with another to run along the side of the cliff at the edge of the city. Rows of tables were set up in the shadows several paces away from where Payton hid. The smell of cooking meat drifted to where they stood. The tables closest to a fire pit were filled with a dozen men. A boy walked plates of food to a few of them before turning around to fetch more.

Across the street from the diners stood a group of people watching, as if desperate to gain sustenance from the smell in the air. Hungry people were nothing new in the city, but it angered him every time he witnessed it. One food simulator would easily feed the starving crowd.

"I hate the Federation," Fiora said through gritted teeth. "Promise me when we figure out how to stop this disaster, we're going to help them. All of them. Promise we won't stop until this nightmare is over for them."

"You have my word," Jaxx said. She didn't need to illicit the promise from him. He'd already been working on that, but he saw how important it was for her to lay voice to it. He could imagine how she felt was much like the first time he'd seen such misery.

A few of the men at the dining tables taunted those who begged for food. He knew the hungry would not cross the street. To do so would be to draw the ridicule of those who were fed.

Jaxx continued walking, waiting to explain things further until they were out of sight. They arrived at the hanging material.

"Some of them are just children," Fiora said. "I know the cruelty that exists in the universes, but to see it..."

Payton pulled back a sheet and said, "We send them to the corner to stare at the food so no one suspects they're getting fed from another source. If they stopped showing, someone would notice. A runner will come by later. With Brogan gone the food runs are taking longer."

Jaxx nodded when Fiora glanced at him. Payton had beat him to the explanation. "It's true."

Fiora sighed in relief.

"Doyen is with his followers at the tables. This is as close as we can get without being in full view." Payton held the material aside so they could duck underneath. "Hopefully, the sheets will provide some protection."

"This will do," Fiora agreed.

"I'll go tell Salena and Grier what we're doing. We'll be nearby if anything happens." Payton slipped through the laundry and disappeared into a passing group.

"Can you use your shifter eyesight and tell me which one he is?" Fiora asked.

Jaxx focused his vision. It didn't take him long to pick Doyen out of the gathering. "Back to the cliff, closest to the cooking fire facing the others."

Fiora took a deep breath, angling her head as material blew in front of their view. "Got him."

"Say the word," Jaxx said.

"I know." She smiled at him. Her eyes already looked tired, and she hadn't even started the reading. "You'll fly me out of here."

"Yes." He nodded.

"There is something you can do for me." Fiora touched his cheek.

"Anything."

"When I start, don't touch me and bring me out of my visions. My nose will bleed and I'll be in pain, but don't stop it. This is too important." Fiora ran her thumb along his bottom lip. "I know you'll want to, but don't."

Jaxx didn't like it, but he nodded once before dipping slightly to kiss her lips. Her hand slid against his cheek in a gentle caress. He covered her hand with his, holding her to him for a little while longer before finally letting go.

16

THE ROCKS STARTED WITH A LIGHT TRICKLE down the side of the cliff to her left. Fiora forced herself not to react in fear, even though she wanted to throw her hands protectively over her head before larger stones rained down on her. The material changed before lighting up in flames from the explosion. The fire burned all around her. She pushed past the blistering heat. This is not the moment she needed to see.

She focused her eyes on Doyen's short black hair, ignoring the material that blew past her to hide him in an unrhythmic pattern. As she stared at him, his blue eyes came into focus. Not so much that her eyesight improved over the distance, but because she picked up on his timeline.

Ash began to fall. Doyen's gaze was cold, a reflection of his dead emotions. She'd sensed his kind before. It showed in their expressions, their manners, in their speech. People like him felt very little, and what they did feel was only for themselves—their need for adoration, their wants and desires. He was the kind who could easily kill thousands if it advanced his agenda...or if he simply had a bad day and felt like taking it out on others.

But capable did not mean he was the one. Fiora needed to see the moment the disaster started.

Many acts of violence formed Doyen's future. They came at her in flashes. She flinched as she watched the man strike down a young boy for daring to bump into him. Crowds became inflamed as he spoke of attacking shifters. His men pulled a woman off the streets and brought her to him. Fiora felt the bile rising in her as she watched the horror that ensued. When Doyen finished, her naked, dead body was thrown in a trash fire by a man in red boots.

"Fiora?" Jaxx's voice felt far away. She managed to lift her hand to keep him back. He couldn't stop this. She had to look. She was the only one who could.

Next, the smell of liquor overwhelmed her senses, and she coughed as it burned her lungs. She felt as if she moved through a campsite in the forest. Large cats slept on the ground on old blankets next to messy piles of men's clothing. A giant metal canister, which seemed to be the source of the smell, had been situated between them. Doyen ordered his men to attack, watching as they obeyed. The cat-shifters never had a chance as they were slaughtered in their sleep.

Each second felt like an eternity in the fire pits of Bravon. Doyen and his men were so proud of what they had done. Fiora wanted to scream at them to stop but couldn't.

A bright light illuminated the forest, interrupting the post-massacre celebration. The world spun as her viewpoint altered to face the other direction. The eruption over Shelter City could be seen even miles away.

"What is this? What are you doing in here?" an angry voice demanded.

The angry voice jolted her away from the forest vision. She turned to look only to be smacked in the face by something that was on fire. Startled and disoriented, Fiora gasped and flung her hands to stop the attack. The fire disappeared, and she ended up tangled in a wet cloth.

"You're getting blood on my linens. Get out, get

out!" A man charged at her with a smooth wooden bat. Red, blistered skin covered his face.

The man swung at her. Fiora screamed, unable to focus between the future and the present.

Jaxx jumped in front of her and caught the bat in his hand. With a growl, he pushed the man away from them. The man fell on the ground.

Jaxx grabbed her hand. Instantly the fire cleared, and she saw that the man staring at her from the ground no longer had blisters.

Jaxx tossed the bat aside. "Go!"

The man scrambled away from them.

"Don't worry. He won't hurt you." Jaxx grabbed the damp cloth she'd been entangled in and lifted a corner to clean her face gently. She glanced down to see blood staining the front of her shirt.

"Hey! What's going on in there?"

Fiora pushed the cloth away from her face and turned toward the sound. Doyen and his men had stood at the commotion and came to investigate.

"We have to leave." Fiora grabbed Jaxx's hand and pulled him behind her as she pushed her way out of the material. She rushed in the opposite direction of the dining tables, hoping to get lost in the crowd. She found Payton watching from across the street.

"What did you see?" Jaxx asked, threading his arm behind her back to propel her forward.

"It wasn't him. He will be in the forest slaughtering cat-shifters when the explosion goes off." Fiora's head pounded, and she felt dizzy.

"What?" Jaxx slowed and glanced back as if his first reaction was to help the cat-shifters.

"Stop them!" Doyen yelled.

"It wasn't him," Fiora was forced to repeat. "He will be in the forest slaughtering cat-shifters when the explosion goes off."

"There you are." Payton showed up next to her. She swept a cloak around Fiora's shoulders. "Jaxx, we have to split up. That launderer is under Doyen's protection. They're looking for a man and woman together. We'll meet you back at Yevgen's."

Jaxx's grip tightened on her hand. "No, I can get you both out of here."

"Jaxx, you can't shift here. The Federation cannot see us in the city. It will undo all the progress we've made." Payton pulled at Fiora's arm, trying to get him to let go.

Fiora wanted to reassure him but couldn't. In truth she didn't know if it would be all right. "I think we need to listen to Payton. Doyen is dangerous. We can't get into a fight with him here. He has too many followers."

"Don't stop walking," Jaxx ordered Payton. "Get her out of this crowd."

"I'll protect her with my life," Payton answered.

"I'm…" Jaxx's words were lost as more shouts sounded.

Doyen's men began pushing over tables and terrorizing the crowd. "Where are they? Find them!"

Jaxx finally released her hand. "I love you. I'm right behind you."

"I love you," Fiora answered.

Timelines came at her from all directions. After focusing on Doyen, she found it difficult to block out the onslaught of visions. She saw a man kissing a woman in a stolen embrace, only to have the ghost of the image replaced by children running through them.

Ash again fell like snow. Payton had a hold of her elbow and was guiding her through the city. Fiora wanted to turn and look for Jaxx, but she couldn't see past the flurry of movement as visions overlaid reality. Several people ran down the street, screaming. Their translucent forms passed over two unaware children playing some kind of game in the dirt.

"We're drawing attention." Payton paused long enough to pull the cloak over Fiora's head. "You look like I beat you bloody. Try not to glance up."

Fiora saw a future where Payton was curled into a ball crying surrounded by darkness. She felt a wave of anguish wash over her from the woman.

"I'm sorry," Fiora whispered in reaction to the pain.

"Not your fault," Payton answered, clearly not understanding what Fiora referred to.

Before she could explain, the ash stopped falling. Fiora looked to the sky, waiting for the explosion. It didn't come. Something prickled her senses.

Fiora pushed the cloak off her head and looked around the city street. A myriad of sounds from the murmur of conversation to a high-pitched laugh overtook her hearing.

"*Du—o!*" In the chaos of the present and future, a figure caught her notice. She smelled the faint trace of liquor from the forest.

"Come—" Payton began.

"No, wait." Fiora dug in her heels and refused to follow.

The figure looked like so many others in the city. His eyes were rimmed with red, and he weaved on his feet. His mouth opened, and he angrily shouted something. Fiora tried to focus on his words.

"*Du—o!*"

Fiora focused harder, making the moment replay itself.

"*Dulla! Where are you, woman?*" The figure moved past them, and the smell became stronger. "*Stupid whore. I'll show you.*"

Fiora pointed away from where Payton led them. "We have to go down there."

"The alley? Many of them don't come out on the other side. They're dead ends. I don't know what's back there." Payton shook her head. "Yevgen is this way. I need to get you out of the crowds."

The princess again tried to correct their path.

"Trust me," Fiora insisted, forcing Payton to walk with her since the woman wouldn't let go of her. "This way."

"If you say so." Payton didn't sound sure, but she darted ahead of Fiora to enter the alleyway first.

The visions happening in the alley were less active than the wider street. Fiora ignored the numerous future-trysting couples against the metal walls. The figure she was interested in was the man walking away from them.

The walkway was between the buildings with no doors on either side. The uneven width caused them to turn to the side to pass a few times. Old glass bottles and scrap metal littered the ground.

"Where are we going?" Payton asked.

"I don't know. Follow him," Fiora answered, pointing after the man.

"Follow who?" Payton glanced back at her. "There's no one there."

"Me. Follow me." Fiora touched Payton's arm to move her out of the way so she could take the lead.

Adrenaline pumped through her, and she found a renewed strength. The smell of liquor became more potent, the closer she came to the vision. Dulla's drunken husband mumbled to himself, cursing his wife for running off, threatening to kill Brogan if he ever dared to show his face. Fiora already knew that the brother and sister would not be returning to Shelter City.

After what felt like a long walk, the figure finally stopped at a dead end. One of the metal canisters like the cat-shifters had in the forest stood in the small opening. The smell of liquor was stronger here.

"What is it?" Payton asked, clearly not seeing what Fiora did.

"Liquor," Fiora tried to explain, but it was hard to concentrate between the future and Payton's present. Dulla's husband fussed with the metal canister. Loud clanks came from his work.

"You need a drink?" Payton asked. "I'm all for it, but there are better places than tapping into this old still."

"Still?"

"Yeah." Payton walked up to the metal canister and slapped it. The man in the future didn't react. "One of the marsh farmers must have sold someone this piece of junk. They use them to brew liquor in the forest. Potent stuff. Smells like rocket fuel, tastes like fire, and it'll take the hair off a cat's back."

Fiora looked at the ground. Liquid dripped, adding to the smell.

"Do you see that?" Fiora asked, unable to determine when it was happening.

"What?" Payton looked around the area before glancing upward.

Dulla's husband let loose a long stream of what could only be translated as obscenities. He threw a tool at the metal wall before he began kicking the still, cursing it for not working.

Fiora lunged to grab Payton. "Wait, don't—"

The man kicked the still one last time. The canister ignited. A blast of heat and flames incinerated her flesh. There was no time to cry out, or run, or think. With that one blast, it was over and everything went black.

17

"What happened?" Jaxx's voice broke through the cloak of darkness.

"She insisted I take her down an alley to where someone had hidden an old still, then she just kind of..." Payton hesitated. "I don't know. She went all pale and limp."

"I told you to bring her straight here. She can't control the visions," Jaxx said.

"Scans indicate she's fine," Yevgen said. "No significant blood loss."

As she struggled to find her way out of the darkness, she knew Jaxx was touching her to stop the visions. A light moan escaped her lips as she tried to tell him she was alive.

"Fiora?" Jaxx kneeled beside her on a cot behind

Yevgen's partition of monitors. The soft blue light illuminated his face.

Payton stood behind him with her lips pressed firmly together.

"I found it," Fiora said, her voice rough. She coughed and tried to sit.

"Take it easy." Jaxx urged her to stay down.

A bruise had formed on the side of his jaw, barely discernable in the dim lights. She lifted her hand to turn his face. "What happened?"

"It's nothing. Tiny brawl," he dismissed.

"Tiny brawl?" Fiora arched a brow. "I can't tell you how annoying it is that other people can pick and choose what they tell me."

"Doyen's men got a little rowdy. Grier and I handled it." Jaxx obviously tried to hide it, but he couldn't help his small smile. "Since we can't shift in the city without causing an incident, we had to absorb a few of the blows." His smile grew a little wider. "We won."

"Salena?" Fiora asked. This time she did push up from the cot to peer between the monitors.

"Safe," Payton said, "but she aggravated her ankle. Grier is sneaking her out of the city and is flying her to a medical booth."

"I told her to watch where she landed." Fiora

closed her eyes and took a deep breath. Maybe laying down was better. Her head throbbed.

"Payton, grab the handheld medic. It should be in the pack we brought with us," Jaxx said.

"What happened? What did you see?" Payton asked as she went to retrieve the bag. She sat on the floor and began digging through it.

"It's Dulla's husband." Fiora eased back down on the cot. It wasn't the most comfortable of beds, but she was in no position to be picky.

"What is Dulla's husband?" Jaxx asked.

"The cause of the disaster," Fiora answered, again closing her eyes. She draped a hand over her eyelids to make it even darker. Her head pounded less in the black. "The one scenario we didn't consider, Jaxx, was sending Dulla back to Shelter City. If we had, we might have stopped this without realizing it. With his pregnant wife abandoning him and everyone knowing about it, the man will fall into bitterness. There is no one here to temper his actions."

"I would have placed a thousand space credits on it being Doyen," Payton admitted. She sighed as she closed the pack and stood to drop it to the side out of the way. "I don't see the handheld in here."

Jaxx frowned. "Maybe they left it by the watchtower before we entered the city. Or maybe Grier needed it for Salena."

Fiora flinched, remembering Doyen's timeline. She ignored the missing handheld because she didn't have an answer as to its location. Doyen's story continued to flow out of her. "Doyen is evil, pure evil, but not the cause of the destruction. I saw him at the time of the explosion. He was in the forest with some of his men killing cat-shifters as they slept. I think they were going to steal their still."

"Marsh farmers," Payton said. "You were talking about that in the alley before you fainted."

"Liquor would be like liquid currency," Jaxx said. "It's no wonder they want a way to produce it."

"And food," Fiora whispered, trying not to remember the intent she'd felt in Doyen. She dropped her hand away from her eyes. "The shifters were in their cat forms."

Payton made a strange choking noise and covered her mouth. She turned away from them and took several deep breaths. After a moment, she said, "Some of the marsh farmers can be real space cadets to deal with, but they don't deserve that."

Fiora nodded. "I recognized some of the men with him in the forest. After people escape the destroyed city, they will be responsible for many of the murders I see happening afterward."

"We have time to stop it now, thanks to you," Jaxx said. "None of that is going to happen."

"So this husband blows up the city as revenge against people laughing at him for his wife leaving?" Payton asked.

"No, as a mistake. He has that old still. I think he's selling liquor or trying to. He tries to repair it, but he's drunk and angry, and instead...*boom*." Unable to get comfortable, Fiora tried to sit up. Again it was a mistake, and she had to settle back down.

"Do we even know his name?" Payton asked.

This time Fiora laid on her side. "I didn't even know what he looked like until I saw him today. When we found Dulla in the forest with her brother the husband was in her past, not her future. I had no way of seeing him."

"Dulla's husband is named Lorman," Yevgen called, signifying he was eavesdropping. "Local drunk. Violent tendencies."

"Are you sure it's him?" Payton asked.

"Yes, fairly. He was mumbling about her leaving him right before the accident." Fiora pressed her fingers to her temple.

Jaxx stroked back her hair while keeping hold of

her hand. "We'll take care of this. I promise. For now, you just need to rest."

"Wait a minute..." Payton went around to the other side of the partition. "Yevgen, where is it?"

"Where is what, my love?" Yevgen answered from the other side of the screens.

"The handheld. Where is it?" she demanded.

"Nothing in Shelter City is free," Yevgen said. "I gave you the information."

Fiora could see Payton at the edge of the monitors. "So you stole from the pack? That's not trading. That's thievery."

"It made such a beautiful little humming noise, calling to me," Yevgen protested.

"Yevgen, I will gladly let you keep it as an information trade if you let me use it to help Fiora," Jaxx said.

"Deal." Yevgen's sling slid on the metal casters as he zoomed past them, forcing Jaxx to lean back so he didn't get smacked by the man's hanging backside. He went to the wall and lifted a square piece of metal. When he glided back to them, he held the medic unit. "Here you go."

"We're going to have a talk about stealing," Payton told him sternly.

Yevgen gave the handheld to Jaxx before spinning around to face Payton. He reached for her. "You know my circuits can't tolerate it when you're mad at me."

Jaxx ignored the cyborg as he turned on the unit. "Touch my arm."

"I'm sorry I'm so tired." Fiora slipped her fingers from his grasp and moved them down his arm to maintain contact. "There are so many timelines here."

Jaxx programmed the device and then held it to her temple. "This should help you sleep. You'll be safe here. Payton and I will take care of that still. Everything is going to be all right."

Fiora opened her mouth to answer but was no match for the medicine as it lulled her into darkness.

18

"IF ANYTHING HAPPENS TO HER..." JAXX LET HIS words trail off as he pointed at Yevgen. When he found out he'd been hiding the handheld while Fiora was in pain, Jaxx had wanted to throw the rolling cyborg into the nearest wall.

"I'll guard her with my life," Yevgen promised. "No one will touch her."

"See that you do," Jaxx said, "because your life depends on it."

"Yevgen is on our side, Jaxx," Payton soothed. "Fiora is safe here. And, thanks to her, the people of Shelter City will live to escape another day. She did an amazing thing."

Jaxx gazed at Fiora, afraid to let go of her. With his shifted eyesight, he saw her face clearly. Blood still stained her face. It had dried on her shirt but he could detect its scent. He didn't want the evil she had seen to invade her dreams. Still, he knew he couldn't keep touching her and take care of the exploding still at the same time. He'd promised her that he'd help the people of Shelter City, and that was what he intended to do.

"She is an amazing woman," Jaxx answered at length. "I could not survive without her."

He placed Fiora's hand next to her and let go. She didn't stir, and he hoped the medicine he'd given her helped her to rest dreamlessly.

"I am pleased to see you have found your mate," Payton said. "For all that you do for others, you deserve some happiness for yourself, Jaxx."

"As do you," Jaxx answered. He gave one last glance at Fiora before following Payton out of the cyborg's secret hideaway.

"The way my life is going, I doubt marriage is in my future. As we speak an alien dignitary is trying to negotiate with my father for my hand in marriage to some prince." Payton chuckled. "When I snuck away from the palace, Uncle Quinn was doing his best to keep my father from tearing off the man's head for daring to suggest it."

"Again?" Jaxx chuckled. "I feel a little sorry for

the man you fall in love with. I would not want to face Commander Falke in such a capacity."

"I hope destroying the still works." Payton's voice became serious once more as she turned to the side to pass through the narrow opening. "I didn't want to say anything in front of Fiora, but I don't think she should ever come back here. The look on her face when she stared at me, the horror in her expression, the blood streaming down her chin... Jaxx, it was terrifying. When she fainted, I thought she'd died. I've never seen anyone look at me the way she did. It was as if she couldn't see me. I didn't know what to do to help her."

"I know." Jaxx had seen Fiora's reactions for himself. His connection to her was such that he felt the deep pain radiating off her. "When this is over, I'm taking her somewhere safe and secluded, away from the world. She's sacrificed enough for others, and I worry at what cost to herself."

"I think that's a good idea. I'll do whatever I can to help." Payton stopped at the entrance to Yevgen's passageway. "I'll bring you supplies as you get settled with her, so you don't have to leave her. We have to keep her away from people."

"Thank you." Jaxx hadn't fully formulated his plan and wouldn't until he had a chance to talk to

Fiora about it first. He would give her whatever life she chose.

"Try not to draw attention," Payton said. "After that *tiny* brawl, I'm sure Doyen and his men will be looking for you. I'm not going to be the one to drag your dragon ass back to Fiora if two dozen men decide to overtake us."

Jaxx wasn't worried. He'd seen Payton fight many times. She was quite deadly when forced to bare her claws.

"Please," he drawled. "Everyone knows that dragons are always bailing cats out of danger."

She smirked at his teasing.

Cysgodians moved through the city, each with individual purpose and completely unaware of the peril that unfolded amongst them. They didn't pay attention as Payton and Jaxx slipped from the narrow walkway. If anyone cared to look, they'd probably assume they had ducked away for a sexual encounter, which was common amongst the citizens.

They fell into silence as they moved into the flow of the city streets. He let Payton take the lead as she knew where the still was located. It gave him the chance to keep an eye on her while searching for threats.

A pair of sweeper borgs walked along the street.

Payton changed course and stopped to look at a pile of scrap metal for trade. Jaxx joined her. She pointed toward a jagged piece. The sound of the borgs passed behind them.

"You like what you see?" A woman moved to lift the scrap so they could get a better look.

"Wrong size," Payton dismissed, moving away.

"How about you?" the shopkeeper asked.

"She's the boss." Jaxx followed Payton.

She led him to another narrow passage between buildings. Jaxx frowned. The city's secret byways were not made for a man of his size but this one was a little wider than the one they just came from. The dirt on the ground appeared less traveled the deeper they walked. The metal walls create an effective barricade on each side. There were no doors in which to escape. His foot bumped into a bottle on the ground, sending it rolling.

"Shh," Payton scolded with a flick of her hand.

At first, he thought she scolded him over the bottle, but then he detected the murmur of hushed voices coming from ahead.

"Did you get it?"

"Almost."

"Lorman won't know what hit him."

"Nice and roasty. Filet of traitor."

"Let this be a warning to those who would cross us. There's only one supplier in town."

Payton's eyes flashed as she looked at him. She mouthed, "Doyen."

Jaxx nodded. The space was too small for a fully shifted dragon and cat, but that didn't mean they couldn't half shift. City eyes wouldn't see them here.

Fur sprouted on Payton's face and arms. The silver-white covered every inch of flesh. Her mouth pulled forward, and her pupils became vertical slits. Sharp claws grew from her fingertips. She stood as a woman-cat, caught between a full cat-shift and human.

Jaxx let the hard armor of the dragon cover his flesh. He too half shifted and stood as a man-dragon. Talons extended from his hands, and his teeth sharpened.

The passageway came to a dead ·end. The only way out was the direction they'd come or straight up into the sky. Since Jaxx was the only one who could grow wings, there was no escape for Doyen and his men.

Doyen and two of his followers stood beside a rusted still. A barrel-chested thug had his arms crossed over his chest. Burn scars covered the neck and face of the other, with the variegated flesh changing the shape of his nose and left eye.

A third follower laid on his back, working to sabotage the device. Liquor dripped on the ground next to his muddy red boots. "Pass me the wrench."

At their entrance, Doyen stepped back and pulled two blades from his waist. Barrel instantly dropped his arms and hulked his way toward Jaxx. Burn grabbed the laser wrench from on top of the still and charged Payton.

Barrel swept his arms inward to pound Jaxx's shoulders from both directions. The movement carried with it the sound of landcraft hydraulics. Jaxx grunted as pain shot through him at the man's inhuman strength. If not for the dragon armor, his bones would have cracked under the impact. He drew his hands upward and thrust out, reversing Barrel's attack.

Payton inhaled sharply. The unmistakable smell of blood hit Jaxx. He saw Payton move in the corner of his vision and didn't take his attention away from the brute before him. She was still standing and would call out if she needed him.

Barrel's long-sleeve shirt made it difficult to tell, but as they exchanged blows, Jaxx quickly began to suspect the man's arms were bionic with tubes and metal replacing bone and muscle beneath synthetic skin. Barrel's chest felt like punching stone, and each swing of the man's fist crashed into Jaxx like the blast from a spaceship.

Payton roared and slashed her claws.

"Kill them," Doyen ordered.

Barrel laughed and brought his fist down to crush Jaxx's skull. Jaxx darted to the side and stabbed his talons into the man's neck. He ripped wiring, slicing the synthetic flesh. The man's arm dropped as blood and bionic fluid flowed from the wound. Soon Barrel was on both knees, appearing stunned that he'd been beaten.

Payton had Burn on his back, claws extended. The third follower had scrambled to his feet and leaped for Payton's arm to stop her.

Doyen came at Jaxx with both blades, keeping him from helping Payton. Jaxx's arms were heavy from Barrel's heavy blows. His shoulder popped when he lifted his arm but he ignored the pain. Doyen's knife sliced into Jaxx's forearm.

Jaxx grunted as he grabbed the man's wrist and flung him over his head. Doyen crashed into the metal wall. The sound he made reverberated over the small enclosure.

Jaxx surged toward Payton, sweeping his leg to

kick Burn in the stomach to stop his advance as she handled Red Boots. Burn fell against the still, knocking it over. Both Jaxx and Payton gasped as it fell, freezing for a second as it hit the ground. Thankfully, there was no explosion.

"Finish it," Jaxx told her.

Red Boots grabbed a metal plate he'd taken from the still's control panel and flung it toward Payton like a weapon. She jerked her head to the side. It whizzed past her and embedded into the wall. As she started to right herself, Red Boots lunged. She again ducked to the side. The man flew right past her to skewer himself on the lodged panel. It severed an artery, and he dropped to the ground but not before spraying Payton with blood.

Doyen pushed up and came up at Jaxx with both weapons. Jaxx grabbed the man's wrists, feeling the bones snap as he turned the blades toward their owner. Doyen's inertia threw his body into his weapons. He gurgled in surprise.

Payton and Jaxx turned in unison to fight off Burn only to find he remained where he had fallen. His neck was at an odd angle, and he gasped a couple of times before wheezing a last breath.

For a long moment, they stood, hearts beating hard as they waited to make sure the fight was over.

"Are you all right?" Jaxx asked, holding the cut on his arm.

"That cursed black hole hit me with a wrench." Payton rubbed her forehead. "You?"

"Don't suppose you can tie this up for me?" Jaxx lifted his arm.

Payton reached for the bottom of his tunic shirt and used her claw to tear off a jagged strip. She quickly wrapped it around his forearm to stop the bleeding.

"Thanks." Jaxx flexed his hand.

"Where the hell did Doyen find a bionic soldier?" Payton frowned. She leaned over Barrel and sliced his shirt to look at the muscles beneath. She pressed at his chest and moved toward his shoulder. "Both arms it looks like."

"Probably legs too," Jaxx assumed.

"You can pull off his pants and look, but I'm good." Payton stood. She frowned, not enjoying the thought as she added, "I hate to suggest it, but we should bring the bionic pieces to Yevgen. He can use them for parts. Maybe he can make himself a new pair of legs and we can get future credits on information trades."

"Good idea." Jaxx did not look forward to lugging the large man through the city. "We'll need a cart if we're going to move him. And a shovel. This looks like as good of a resting place as any."

"Agreed." She nudged Doyen with her foot. "You know someone is only going to take over where this one left off."

"That's a battle for another day," Jaxx said. "For now, let's get rid of this mess. I'm ready for this to be over so I can take my bride home."

19

FIORA STOOD WITH JAXX AT THE TOP OF THE watchtower, looking over Shelter City from an opening that served as a perch for the dragons to enter. There was a stack of clothing for the dragons to use so that they could dress if they did not have clothes with them. He told her Olena had constructed such towers all over the Draig kingdom for the flying dragons. Thankfully so, since Fiora now wore one of the shirts to replace her bloody one.

The Federation building seemed so close, and yet so far, on the other side of the cliff. Below them was the place they had first met—she had been dressed like a morphed pleasure droid, and he had been completely naked after a shift. It felt so long ago. So much had happened since the night of her escape.

"Are you ready to look?" he asked.

The last thing she remembered before she'd awakened out of the city was resting on Yevgen's cot, trying not to jostle her head as pain radiated behind both eyes. Jaxx had yet to let go of her.

"It is difficult to believe that it could be over." Fiora looked at the tops of the buildings from their vantage point.

Jaxx told her how he and Payton had gone after the still and had fought with Doyen. She tried to locate where it had been. From this angle, all the buildings appeared very much the same.

"So Doyen really was responsible for the deaths. He and his followers rigged the still to explode." Fiora sighed and leaned into him as Jaxx held her. She loved the feel of his chest as it lifted and fell against her in a steady rhythm.

As far as she was concerned, this moment could last forever. The loud whoosh of the wind against the open window muffled all sounds from outside. The cold air from being high off the ground contrasted to the warmth of Jaxx's embrace. It was only the two of them, away from the world, safe and alone.

"Considering what you saw, I don't think they knew it would cause such a big explosion, but yes, he was responsible. Thanks to you, we were able to stop him." Jaxx leaned back so he could study her face. "You did an amazing thing, Fiora."

She took a deep breath. "We'll see."

Fiora let go of him and stepped closer to the window. The cold hit her, blowing the tunic shirt against her. Goosebumps rose on her body as she forced herself to ignore the weather.

Timelines formed as she stared at the city, but they were nothing like the chaotic mess of before. There were no screams, no explosions, no ash falling like snow over the land. The visions caused the expected discomfort, but nothing like the agonizing pain of before. The memories of what they had prevented would always be there in her head, but at least now they were only a tale of what could have been.

"You're smiling," Jaxx said. "Does that mean it worked?"

A tear slipped over her cheek, and she nodded. "The fire and ash are gone."

Her eyes moved over the city, following pieces of the lives to be lived below. So many people with futures now. They would not all be fantastic stories, but at least they were stories.

"You did well ridding them of Doyen. There was evil in that man, the kind of evil you can't cure. The things I saw him do to women, to children, to *everyone* around him." Fiora hated those images but could take comfort that they too were from a timeline that had changed. "You saved many."

"*We* saved many," he corrected.

Fiora reached for him, and he instantly took her hand. All visions cleared to be replaced by the landscape.

Seeing a dark figure in the sky, she squinted and leaned out the window to try to get a better view. The wind whipped her hair against her face, obstructing it instead.

"Who is that?" she asked.

Jaxx looked toward the sky. His eyes filled with gold as he focused his sight. "Grace."

Fiora watched as Grace circled over them, disappearing behind the tower only to reappear. She lifted her hand, waving at her. Grace again disappeared from view. A loud thump sounded on the roof as Grace landed over them.

Jaxx reached for the stack of shirts and handed one to Fiora. "She'll need this."

"How will she get down?" Fiora asked.

Jaxx pulled Fiora away from the window. He averted his gaze.

A very human, naked Grace dropped down from

above, swinging her legs into the window. She landed in a crouch. When her head lifted, Fiora instantly gave her the tunic shirt to put on.

Grace's hand was balled in a fist as she held the shirt against her chest without putting it on. "We were worried. I flew past Grier carrying Salena into the palace. Aunt Olena sent me to look for you two since you hadn't been back."

"We just finished in the city. We're heading back soon," Jaxx said.

"Did it work?" Grace asked.

"Yes." Fiora nodded.

"We stopped it," Jaxx added.

Grace let loose a long breath. "That is great news indeed. Dulla gave birth to two boys. She didn't make it, but I have a feeling you already know that."

"I'm sorry I didn't tell you," Fiora said.

"I'm sure you had your reasons." Grace looked haunted by what she'd been through with Dulla, but she didn't say anything more about it. "Anyway, while I was in the mountains, I picked this up for you."

Grace tossed a pouch toward Jaxx. He caught it with one hand.

"Shut your eyes," she told her cousin.

Jaxx obeyed, and Grace dropped the shirt. She

smiled at Fiora. "I'm glad you made it out of there in one piece."

"Thank you." Fiora started to say more but Grace turned and propelled herself out of the window.

Fiora's heart leaped in her chest as she ran to watch as Grace's human body dove toward the ground. The dragon ripped from her flesh and before she crashed, her wings pumped hard to carry her into the sky.

"By all the stars, that made my heart jump into my throat," Fiora said. "I guess I still need to get used to the whole flying family thing."

"Grace likes to show off." Jaxx tugged on her hand to get her to turn around.

She smiled, moving to face him. A soft light covered his face, and she glanced at his hand. "What did she give you?"

Jaxx held up a glowing crystal between two fingers. "Proof of what we already knew."

"Is that...?" Fiora reached for it, curious to see the mythical stone she'd heard so much about. The crystal felt like it hummed with energy in her hand, she peered into its depths, mesmerized. "It's beautiful."

"Not as beautiful as you," Jaxx said.

"So this means we're married?" She grinned up at him.

"We will be as soon as you break it," he answered.

Fiora frowned and held it against her chest. "But it's pretty. I was hoping I could keep it."

"Doesn't work like that." He stroked her cheek. "When you break my crystal, it's a symbol that we're joined forever. You accept me, and I accept you. Our fates and our souls become intertwined. My life becomes yours."

"And my life will also become yours?" She smiled, liking the romantic notion.

"Yes, but literally my life becomes yours. When a dragon finds a mate, we share our long years with them. We will live for a very long time. Together. We'll be able to speak without words, share our emotions. You'll be able to tell what I'm thinking. I'll hear you call for me over a distance, and you'll hear me. We'll be joined."

Fiora looked down at the crystal. "All that power is in here?"

Jaxx nodded. "What do you say, Fiora? Marry me. Make me your forever."

The beauty of the stone paled compared to the life and love he offered. She lifted her arm and threw it as hard as she could against the tower wall. It shattered on impact. She felt a lightness to her chest the second the glowing stopped.

"I feel you," she whispered. "Inside me."

Jaxx drew her toward him and grinned. "Not yet, but you will soon, wife."

The promise in his golden eyes caused a shiver to run through her. She felt him as sure as she felt herself—his love, his desire, his need to be with her. It was intoxicating.

Jaxx slid his hand along her hip to dip under the loose shirt. He skated his fingers beneath the material to cup a naked breast. She gasped in pleasure.

Their lips met in a passionate kiss. He pressed her against the wall. She lifted her leg, rubbing it against him while wishing there were no clothes between them.

Fiora tugged at his shirt, wanting to feel more of him. Jaxx leaned away and peeled the shirt from his chest. She kicked off her boots and pushed her pants from her legs.

Jaxx tugged his pants down his hips to reveal his aroused cock. He came back to her and lifted her off the floor. His hands settled on her hips, and Fiora held onto his shoulders for support.

Her body tightened in anticipation. She wanted him inside her. Every nerve in her body focused on his touch, his smell, his heat. He was everything to her. Every moment in her life had built to this, to him.

He brought his body to her sex. With a desperate plunge he entered her, sliding deep. She cried out in pleasure. Tears fell down her cheeks, the emotional release more than she could handle.

Jaxx kissed her moist cheek, his lips moving against her skin. The heat of his breath contrasted the cold from the window. His hands tightened on her ass. He thrust inside her, as eager as she to find release. She rocked against him, not caring that the tunic provided little padding against the stone wall.

Pure need took over their frantic movements. A small noise escaped her mouth each time he pushed forward. Release came hard and sure.

"Jaxx," she cried out, trembling into her climax.

"I love you," he whispered against her ear.

Jaxx stiffened. He held himself deep as he met his release. They stayed pressed together for a long moment.

"I never want to let go," she said with a smile. "I love you, too."

Jaxx slowly lowered her to her feet. He rubbed

his hand along her upper thigh. "It's too cold up here for you."

"I don't notice when you hold me." She caressed his face.

"I notice." Jaxx leaned over to pick up her pants from the floor. "I want to take you home."

"To your parents?" she asked.

Jaxx laughed. "No. *Our* home. Do you think I live with my parents?"

Fiora shrugged and laughed. "I don't know."

"We have a house," he assured her. "In the woods. Close to my parents. I have been on my own for many, many years. But I want you to know that because of the visions we can live anywhere you want, away from people, in the mountains, however far you need to go to be free."

Fiora looked at her hands, turning them as if she felt him against her skin. Suddenly she realized he didn't touch her. She gasped and turned to the window and looked out at the city. Everything stayed in the present like when he held her. Only now they weren't making contact.

She thought of the first person that came to mind —the woman Justina who had tried to rescue her from Jaxx. She focused on finding the woman's time-line. The images came forward, flowing as one vision when it should have been a cascade of many. She saw Justina walking through a street, standing on a crate and yelling, tugging her cloak around her as she walked quickly through an alleyway that made her uneasy.

"What is it?" Jaxx joined her. He laced his pants at his hip.

"I can control which timelines I see, and it doesn't hurt like before." Fiora stopped Justina's timeline. "Or if I want to see them."

"How is that possible?" He started to reach for her only to hold back.

Fiora looked toward where she threw the crystal. "It had to have happened when we mated. Whatever effect your touch has on me must have intensified. You balance me somehow."

Jaxx smiled. She felt his love radiating off him. It was more than an expression. She could feel what he felt.

"You are the most amazing person I have ever met." He leaned in to kiss her softly. "I am truly blessed."

Fiora leaned against him and gazed at the city. Jaxx wrapped his arm around her, stroking her arms to keep her warm. She thought of the toothless woman in the market and was able to see bits of her future. The impressions weren't strong, not like when she was close to the person, but they were controllable.

Fiora started to laugh.

"What's so funny?"

"I should have mated to you the second I saw you standing naked in front of this tower." She turned to face him and place her hand on his chest. "Stopping the apocalypse would have been so much easier."

The End

Visit MichellePillow.com
for Qurilixen World details!

KEEP READING!

Keep Reading!
Find out about Jaxx's parents.
Dark Prince (Dragon Lords)

Out of the fire...

Intergalactic thief, Olena Leyton is one of the best space pirates to sail the high skies. Adventure is in her blood. When her crew is scattered in a run from the law and her spaceship explodes into a ball of flames, she is forced to find sanctuary on a bride procurement ship. She poses as a willing mate to one of the alpha males on the primitive alien planet of Qurilixen to elude the bounty hunters pursuing her.

But, marriage isn't something this pirate takes seriously.

Into the flames…

Dragon-shifting Prince Yusef leads a simple life away from the royal palace. He knows from the first moment he sees his fiery temptress that he will possess her and make her his mate for all time. The prince soon learns that playing with fire will always leave a man burned.

With passions that surge as powerful as theirs, he is not willing to give up his bride without a fight.

THE SERIES CONTINUES...

Need more Dragon Lords?

Dragon Lords: Barbarian Prince

What more Cat-Shifters?

Lords of the Var®: The Savage King

**Dragon Lords and *Lords of the Var*®
in Modern Day Earth?**

Captured by a Dragon-Shifter: Determined Prince

**Read all the Dragon Lords and Var books?
Yay, you, keep going!**

Space Lords: His Frost Maiden

WELCOME TO QURILIXEN

QURILIXEN WORLD - FIRST IN SERIES BOOKS

Keep Reading!

Check out these first-in-series books in the different Qurilixen World series installments!

The Qurilixen World is an extensive collection of science fiction and paranormal romance novels by award-winning NYT Bestselling author, Michelle M. Pillow®.

Note: Each book in each series is a stand alone story.

Dragon Lords Series: Barbarian Prince

Dragon Shapeshifter Romance - The original Dragon Lords series' Anniversary Edition

Going undercover at a mass wedding as a bartered bride, Morrigan Blake has every intention of getting off the barbaric alien planet just as soon as the ceremony over. But the next morning, Morrigan discovers her ride left without her and an alien dragon shifter is claiming she's his wife. It's not exactly the story this reporter had in mind. And to make matters worse, the all-to-seductive dragon-shifter alpha male refuses to take no for an answer.

Lords of the Var® Series: The Savage King
Cat-Shifter Romance

Cat-shifting King Kirill knows he must do his royal duty by his people. When his father unexpectedly dies, it's his destiny to take the throne and all of the responsibility that entails. What he hadn't prepared for is the troublesome prisoner that's now his to deal with.

Undercover Agent Ulyssa is no man's captive.

Trapped in a primitive alien forest awaiting pickup, she's going to make the best out of a bad situation... which doesn't include falling for the seductions of an alpha male king.

Dynasty Lords Series: Seduction of the Phoenix

A prince raised in honor and tradition, a woman raised with nothing at all. She wants to steal their most sacred treasure. He'll do anything to protect it, even if it means marrying a thief.

Space Lords Series: His Frost Maiden
Science Fiction Space Pirate Romance

Lady Josselyn of the House of Craven has been betrayed. With her home world on a Florencian moon under attack and her family dead, she finds herself at the mercy of the one who deceived them. There is only one thing left to do—die with honor. But before she can join her family in the afterlife, she must first avenge all that she held dear. Falling in love with a pirate was never in the plan. Evan and his thieving crewmates might have delayed her fate, but they can't stop destiny.

Captured by a Dragon-Shifter Series: Determined Prince

Dragon Shapeshifter Romance

Dragon-shifter Prince Kyran has studied the Earth people and is ready to assimilate. Female shifters are all but going extinct on his planet of Qurilixen, and his people are desperate for mates—so much so they're taking matters into their own hands. What better place to find a mate than Earth? After all, dragon-shifters had come from there centuries ago. Surely a human female would be honored to be selected by one as fine and fierce as himself.

Galaxy Alien Mail Order Brides Series: Spark

Alien Romance

Earth women better watch out. Things are about to heat up.

Mining ash on a remote planet where temperatures reach hellish degrees doesn't leave Kal (aka Spark) much room for dating. Lucky for this hardworking man, a new corporation Galaxy Alien Mail Order Brides is ready to help him find the girl of his dreams. Does it really matter that he lied on his application and really isn't looking for long term, but rather some fast action? Earth women better watch out. Things are about to heat up.

Happy Reading!

MichellePillow.com

ABOUT MICHELLE M. PILLOW

New York Times & *USA TODAY*
Bestselling Author

Michelle loves to travel and try new things, whether it's a paranormal investigation of an old Vaudeville Theatre or climbing Mayan temples in Belize. She believes life is an adventure fueled by copious amounts of coffee.

Newly relocated to the American South, Michelle is involved in various film and documentary projects with her talented director husband. She is mom to a fantastic artist. And she's managed by a dog and cat who make sure she's meeting her deadlines.

For the most part she can be found wearing pajama pants and working in her office. There may or may not be dancing. It's all part of the creative process.

Come say hello! Michelle loves talking with readers on social media!

www.MichellePillow.com

facebook.com/AuthorMichellePillow

x.com/michellepillow

instagram.com/michellempillow

bookbub.com/authors/michelle-m-pillow

goodreads.com/Michelle_Pillow

amazon.com/author/michellepillow

youtube.com/michellepillow

pinterest.com/michellepillow

JOIN THE EXCLUSIVE CLUB!

Join the Pillow Fighters' Reader Club to stay informed about new books, sales, contests, giveaways, exclusive content, preorders and more!

michellepillow.com/author-updates

WE THINK YOU'LL LOVE...

Readers who love this series,
love the Warlocks MacGregors!

Love Potions

*A little magickal mischief never hurt anyone until a
love potion goes terribly wrong.*

Erik MacGregor is from a line of ancient (and
mischievous) Scottish warlocks. He isn't looking for
love. After centuries of bachelorhood, it's not even a
consideration... until he moves in next door to Lydia
Barratt. It's clear the beauty wants nothing to do with
him, but he's drawn to her and determined to win her
over.

The last thing Lydia needs is an alpha male type meddling in her private life. Just because he's gorgeous, wealthy, and totally rocks a kilt doesn't mean she's going to fall for his seductive charms.

Humans aren't supposed to know about his family's magic or the fact he's a cat shifter. It's better if mortals don't know the paranormal exists. But when a family prank goes terribly wrong, causing Erik to succumb to a love potion, Lydia becomes the target of his sudden and embarrassingly obsessive behavior.

They'll have to find a way to pull Erik out of the spell fast when it becomes clear that Lydia has more than a lovesick warlock to worry about.

Warning: Contains yummy, hot, mischievous MacGregors who may or may not be wielding love potion magick in an effort to prank their older brother, and who are almost certainly up to no good on their quest to find true love.

PLEASE LEAVE A REVIEW

THANK YOU FOR READING!

Please take a moment to share your thoughts by
reviewing this book.

Be sure to check out Michelle's other titles at

www.MichellePillow.com